THE SAVIOR OF MILLER'S CROSSING

David Clark

And I heard a great voice out of the temple saying to the seven angels, Go your ways, and pour out the vials of the wrath of God upon the earth.

And the first went, and poured out his vial upon the earth; and there fell a noisome and grievous sore upon the men which had the mark of the beast, and upon them which worshipped his image.

And the second angel poured out his vial upon the sea; and it became as the blood of a dead man: and every living soul died in the sea.

And the third angel poured out his vial upon the rivers and fountains of waters; and they became blood.

And I heard the angel of the waters say, Thou art righteous, O Lord, which art, and wast, and shalt be, because thou hast judged thus.

For they have shed the blood of saints and prophets, and thou hast given them blood to drink; for they are worthy.

And I heard another out of the altar say, Even so, Lord God Almighty, true and righteous are thy judgments.

And the fourth angel poured out his vial upon the sun; and power was given unto him to scorch men with fire.

And men were scorched with great heat, and blasphemed the name of God, which hath power over these plagues: and they repented not to give him glory.

And the fifth angel poured out his vial upon the seat of the beast; and his kingdom was full of darkness; and they gnawed their tongues for pain,

And blasphemed the God of heaven because of their pains and their sores, and repented not of their deeds.

And the sixth angel poured out his vial upon the great river Euphrates; and the water thereof was dried up, that the way of the kings of the east might be prepared.

And I saw three unclean spirits like frogs come out of the mouth of the dragon, and out of the mouth of the beast, and out of the mouth of the false prophet.

For they are the spirits of devils, working miracles, which go forth unto the kings of the earth and of the whole world, to gather them to the battle of that great day of God Almighty.

Behold, I come as a thief. Blessed is he that watcheth, and keepeth his garments, lest he walk naked, and they see his shame.

And he gathered them together into a place called in the Hebrew tongue Armageddon.

And the seventh angel poured out his vial into the air; and there came a great voice out of the temple of heaven, from the throne, saying, It is done.

And there were voices, and thunders, and lightnings; and there was a great earthquake, such as was not since men were upon the earth, so mighty an earthquake, and so great.

And the great city was divided into three parts, and the cities of the nations fell: and great Babylon came in remembrance before God, to give unto her the cup of the wine of the fierceness of his wrath.

And every island fled away, and the mountains were not found.

And there fell upon men a great hail out of heaven, every stone about the weight of a talent: and men blasphemed God because of the plague of the hail; for the plague thereof was exceeding great.

— *Revelation 16*

1

"Jacob Meyer! Get your ass back here." Sylvia chased Jacob through the house with a three-year-old in tow. Jacob slowed up just enough to grab his pack off the dining room table before he went out the door.

"I'll be back later," he called from the front door, and ran to the waiting truck, but then he stopped before he opened the door and sheepishly walked back to the porch where Sylvia was waiting. He leaned forward and kissed her on her waiting cheek and then bent down and hugged Edwin.

"This is all to make your life easier," he said to his son, and he meant it. If someone had taken the time to do all this long before the responsibility passed down to his father and then to him, he would have been grateful.

"Jacob, the washer is acting up. You said you were going to look at it today," Sylvia reminded him.

"And I will. When I get back. Have I ever let you down?"

"No," she said. "That's the problem. You never let anyone down and take on way too much." She looked past Jacob to the truck and gave a wave at the person in the driver's seat. "Morning Edward."

"Morning, Sylvia," Edward responded through the open passenger window.

"I have to do this. You know that."

"I do," she said with a caressing touch to the side of Jacob's face. "Sometimes I would like a Saturday to be ours."

"It's just a few hours, and you know how important this is," Jacob pleaded, and flashed his killer smile at his wife of the last five years.

Sylvia looked down at the floor, then away from him before she conceded. "Go on. Go."

Jacob didn't wait. He gave her another kiss and bounded down the steps to the truck. "Just sit, relax, don't do any laundry."

"Just be careful and leave your shoes out here when you get back. You made a huge muddy mess last time," she called after him.

"Will do, love you honey," Jacob said before the passenger door clanged shut. Sylvia waved as it pulled away, and up and over the rise in the driveway. Jacob watched and waved back until she disappeared.

"Things okay?" Edward asked.

"Yep. The washer is broken. I think the belt is broken, but I already picked up a new one. I'll look at it this afternoon."

"That's not what I meant. Is everything okay?" Edward glanced at his son and then back on the road.

"If you're asking about our marriage. Things are fine."

"Marriage takes work and time, Jacob. Don't let things like this get in the way."

"Dad, it's not. She understands how important this is." Jacob waited for his father to show some acceptance of this answer. Things were fine on that front. Did things interfere from time to time? Of course, and Sylvia knew that when she accepted Jacob's proposal. She was from Miller's Crossing; she knew better than anyone what it meant to be a Meyer in this town. That was probably why she wasn't too upset when Sheriff Taylor burst in on their first anniversary and dragged Jacob with him to help with a new sighting. There was no complaint or admonishment when he returned after two in the morning. No check for booze on his breath or lipstick on his collar. She was there at home, watching television, when he walked in and asked to hear all about it.

"Good," Edward said.

"Plus, we don't have a lot more to cover."

"That's true."

Jacob reached inside his pack and pulled out his logbook and reviewed the last several entries. Where they were heading today was adjoining to the last area they checked. While nothing significant happened there in the past, Jacob had crossed referenced with his father's memory, and noted a few minor events in that general area.

"Let's start on the east side and work west. You had a few encounters just to the east of it, and Sarah and Father Murray had one encounter there too." Jacob held up his hand-drawn map so Edward could glance at it.

"Sounds like a plan," Edward said as they pulled off the road and down a wheel rutted drive that resembled the one that led to Jacob's farmhouse. Up ahead of them waited a simple farmhouse and silo with fields of grain on either side of it. It looked ready to harvest.

They came to a stop up at the farmhouse, and the two men got out. Jack pushed his logbook and pencil into his pocket and threw his bag over his shoulder.

"Thanks for letting us poke around some Leroy," Edward said while waving at the man who stood on the front stoop. Jacob waved to one of his fellow farmers. Leroy Henderson grew grains, so not a competitor, or partner for Jacob, but that didn't matter. Jacob's reputation for what he had done with the old Meyer's family farm had spread quickly across the town and earned the respect of one and all. Jacob making sure he met all the other working farmers in the town didn't hurt either.

"No problem. How much you going to cover today?"

"Going to start just north of the field there," Jacob said, pointing to the large plot of land just to the side of the farmhouse. "Then maybe work as far west as the county line."

"Does this stop right at the line?" asked Leroy.

Jacob didn't know, and he looked at his father, who just shrugged their replies. Jacob doubted what made their town special stopped at some imaginary line on a map.

"Well, I hope you guys find nothing," Leroy said with a laugh. Jacob and Edward passed by him and out into the field, where Jacob pulled out a little collapsible tripod from his bag and set it up on a point at the border of today's target. Then, methodically, they started walking line by line between that point and the furthest point they planned to cover today. Jacob kept his notebook handy, while Edward held another book firmly as he explored.

They were making a map of the entire town. Not one that would tell you how to make it from one house to another or find your way back to the interstate. This was a paranormal map that documented the hot spots where they felt or encountered anything, no matter how small. Jacob had cross-referenced his own experiences with stories from his father and sister and plotted them on the map to create a complete picture.

So far, they had found seventeen places with activity of some type, whether a feeling they experienced when mapping it or other events that occurred over the last few years in the vicinity. The hottest spots were obviously closer to the shed in the woods. Edward was more than a little hesitant to explore that area. Jacob felt the same, but he knew it needed to be done. The more they knew about their town, on this level, the better. Jacob didn't like surprises; and he had had enough of them to last a lifetime.

Of the seventeen places, only four areas were what Jacob called hot spots. Those were spots with frequent problem zones in both the past and present. Each gave him and his father the traditional pin pricks as they walked through them. Jacob had visited each of those sites on his own, hoping to find the center of the problem area, much like the shed out there in the desolate field everyone now called the Scar. Unlike that spot, Jacob never found the center of the other three. With as much activity that occurred near those spots, he felt there had to be an epic center, and if he found it, he could seal it, but after many searches he came up dry.

"Feeling anything?" Edward asked.

"Just the mosquitoes." They were a common foe during their late summer explorations, and at the moment that was all there was out in this field. Jacob even consulted his notes and GPS points he had recorded in his phone from past encounters just to see if they were far enough east, and they were. The origin of those events had to be some place close by, or so he hoped. It could be in any direction, and really any distance. Ghosts had roamed great distances before.

They were on a lap back toward the tripod when Edward's phone rang. Jacob kept walking and logging, figuring he was getting a grocery list or something, but when he heard him reply, "Are you serious?" Jacob knew this was serious.

He stopped and waited for his father to catch up. "What's going on?"

"Lewis has some kids at Walter's creek. He thinks we should come talk to them."

"Let's go. I'm not finding much here, and we can start there and keep working west next week." Jacob shoved the logbook in his bag and headed for the truck, with his father following. As much as they tried to create a cover story for what happened out at the Scar, conspiracy theories ran amok on the internet. Everything from aliens to sasquatch, and even a few thinking it was where Elvis was hiding. Unfortunately, one theory emerged as the most common source of speculation, and it was one way too close to home. Ghosts. Stories emerged, with even a few people claiming to be residents that knew the truth and sold their story to a tabloid news show or a paranormal hunter show. Not a one of them was an actual resident, but that didn't stop people from making treks to check it out on their own. Jacob knew this was just another one of those, but they still needed to check it out and put on the good show.

2

Jacob and his father pulled up to a familiar scene. A bunch of kids, sitting on the ground next to a patrol car with its lights on. Sheriff Taylor stood over them, with his hands locked on his belt. With how the kids, make that teens, looked, they had laid the danger they were in on thick.

Sheriff Taylor quickly learned the script from Lewis Tillingsly when he took the job. Jacob felt he even delivered it better than the former sheriff. With the influx of visitors coming to check out the Scar, just to see if they could find any evidence of the many conspiracy theories published on the internet, they needed a cover story, and one that would, or should, deter people from venturing too close. Lewis Tillingsly, when he was sheriff, borrowed an old rusted out milk tanker from Steven Svenson's, painted it up with a made-up company's name, Nationwide Chemicals, and then used a tractor to knock it on its side right just over where the Walter's Creek bridge used to be.

When Edward pulled the truck to a stop, Lewis opened the passenger door of the cruiser and stepped out. The Meyers did the same, following the script, just as they had so many times before. The two men hadn't walked more than a couple of steps before Edward was chomping in on his first line.

"How far did they get?"

"I saw them, eh... a couple of hundred yards in," responded Lewis.

The script had a decision point in it that depended on that response. If they had only made it as far as the creek, they would have received the soft warning. Maybe a good tongue lashing from the sheriff, but this was something different, and it was a rare path they had to follow. That didn't mean it wasn't well rehearsed, and both Jacob and Edward walked over to Lewis.

"Let me see your eyes," requested Edward.

Lewis reached up and opened each of his eyes while Edward looked. Jacob walked over to the three kids that were sitting beside the cruiser. Two boys, and one girl. All probably somewhere between sixteen and eighteen, a detail that they would be sure to gather as they did their medical history over the course of the next few hours, which Jacob knew none of them would enjoy.

"How are you three feeling?" asked Jacob. He kept his distance from them.

The three looked at each other and didn't respond.

"I'm afraid Doctor Meyer, they appear to have decided to remain silent."

Jacob shook his head and did his best to produce a look of admonishment. All he had to do was try to remember how his father or Father Murray looked at him on the many times he smarted off when he was younger.

"You need to tell me how you feel. Being silent here is the worst decision you could make." Jacob bent down. "I need each of you to open your eyes wide." He looked closely as three puzzled faces looked back at him.

"We're not on drugs."

"We could care less if you were," shot back Jacob. "That really doesn't matter. Do you know what you were just walking through?"

Jacob knew the cadence here. Give them a few seconds to think, but not enough time to respond. "I know what the internet says. Everything from aliens, bigfoot, the lost city of Atlantis, and Hell knows what else. After all these years, I lost track of what the rest of the theories are. The truth is even more horrific than the theories. That chemical out there will eat your flesh off, starting with your eyeballs. Now, I need to see your eyes, and you need to tell me if your skin itches."

Right then, three sets of hands sprung up and explored the exposed skin of their arms and face. Even after delivering that speech, and its many flavors, as many times as Jacob had, he still felt the psychosomatic itching start along his own arms.

"Now hold open your eyes."

One by one they did as Jacob asked and held open their eyes so Jacob could begin the checkup, just like his father was giving Lewis. He could hear the questions he asked, with Lewis responding negatively to each. Then Lewis explained he never really walked out there, just called for the kids to return, and then called the sheriff. This was going according to the script. Jacob looked at their eyes, and then asked each to hold out their arms, palm down first, and then asked them to rotate them. After which, he looked up at Sheriff Taylor. "Have you called for transport?"

"It's on the way."

"Wait...," the first boy panicked. "We aren't going to jail, are we?"

"No, the hospital. We need to run you through a decontamination shower. I see signs of chemical irritation in your eyes and on your arms." This statement always created more panic, and more frantic searching for something that wasn't there, but it always miraculously appeared, causing each of the teens to scratch uncontrollably.

Jacob left when two of the teens started crying and walked back over to his father and Lewis. "I doubt they will venture this way again."

His father nodded.

"The shower will make sure of that," remarked Lewis.

"So, how far did they really make it?" Jacob asked.

"What I said. Not out to the woods, but a good bit out there."

That was what Jacob was afraid of. What came next was not something he, nor his father, looked forward to. They waited for an ambulance to arrive. Two nurses were in the back in full gown and face mask. They helped the teens into the back and then it left for the hospital for a vigorous scrubbing with cold water, what they called decontamination, and a thorough exam. All parts of the illusion that they created, and only used in the most extreme cases, for those that crossed over and into the Scar, or those that appeared to be making some kind of video log of their adventure. The hope was, they would tell others or post about it on the Internet, and it would eventually help squash the rumors and deter others.

Once the ambulance disappeared around the bend, Jacob and Edward moved onto the next, and most dreaded step. Lewis walked them as far as the shore of the creek and stood there watching as Jacob pulled the small aluminum flat-bottom boat they kept hidden under the remains of the bridge. He and his father boarded it and rowed across to the other side. Both men hesitated to step off on the other side. This was a place they had been before, but that didn't mean it was a place they wanted to visit often. Both men would be happy if they never had to visit here again.

Jacob remembered his first contact with this unholy ground. Then it was only with an exploratory paddle from the safety of kayak. This time was less eventful, so far. Two feet were firmly on land, and nothing had happened yet. Either there was nothing, or Jacob's little safety net in his pocket was doing its job. They walked in further across the desolate landscape. Over the years, nothing had grown back. Not a flower, not a tree, or even a weed. It was still nothing but dirt and pulverized downed trees. Edward looked back a few times to check in with Lewis, who was standing on the shore pointing them in the direction he saw the kids. When the sheriff arrived, he ordered them via the loudspeaker on the cruiser to come back immediately, leaving whatever they had with them where they were. This was part of the illusion. Contamination was the excuse, but that was an illusion as well. Jacob and Edward needed to see whatever it was, left where it was, and, more importantly, how it was.

This time, they discovered a common sight. Electromagnetic Field detectors and something sold on the internet called a spirit box. Jacob looked one of those up once. The $300 price tag scared that notion right out of his head. It was just a box with a speaker and some flashing lights. Supposedly, it picked up the voices of the dead and tells you when they are close. The EMF detectors also told you if one is close by, but they will also tell you if you are around bad wiring or a large generator. Jacob would hate to tell them that none of that really works, and you don't need any special electronics to hear ghosts. The talkers are still around, but Jacob mostly leaves those alone, unless they are causing issues. The good news, they found no signs of any type of ceremony which they have found before. It appeared this time was nothing beyond just some curious souls that were hoping to find evidence of life after death. Jacob wondered what they would really think if they knew what he did.

Edward and Jacob gathered up the equipment to add to their collection of things locked away and headed back. Each taking a moment or two to feel around for anything, but it was all really quiet, which it had been since Jacob's last visit to the shed. He knew his father told him it was a cycle, but each day of silence that passed by further fortified his belief that he had sealed it. Father Murray cautioned him many times. A day in the world isn't even a second in the grand scheme of things.

Jacob held the items up for Lewis to see just before they climbed back into the boat. He shook his head, headed back up to the road, as the two men paddled back over.

"The normal," Edward reported as they walked up to the road, and then threw the items into the back of the truck. "Everything is quiet."

"Those kids are going to be hating life. That water they use at the hospital is freezing." Lewis said with a chuckle. It was all part of the illusion meant to send a message. Only time would tell if it worked.

3

"I know. I know. The washing machine." Jacob said as he walked through the house, depositing his bag back on the dining room table, which had become its home when not in use.

"First your shoes," corrected Sylvia.

Jacob didn't have to see it. He knew her eyes were rolling when he passed her on his way back to the front door to put his shoes out on the porch. They really weren't muddy at all, but rules were rules, and Sylvia liked to keep a neat house. If only she had seen this place when he, his father, and Sarah arrived almost twenty years ago. Time had painted everything in dust. Of course, what place wouldn't be a little dusty after almost thirty years?

On his way back through, he scooped up his son and threw him up on his shoulders. "Let's go fix that washer."

His son, Edwin, let out a squeal.

"Duck", Jacob said, as they walked through the kitchen door. Just to be sure, Jacob ducked himself to make sure his son didn't come close to the top of the door. Once they were out on the back porch, he sat his son down and handed him his own toolbox, complete with a plastic screwdriver and hammer. Edwin immediately began unscrewing the washer's front plate. Jacob hated to tell his son he was going to have a hard time doing that, seeing that he wasn't anywhere close to any true screws or points of attachment. It occupied him, and he seemed to enjoy it. That was all that mattered to Jacob; at least partially. What also mattered was fixing the washing machine. Jacob hoped it was really just the belt. He picked up a spare from the store yesterday.

He got his answer, and a little fright, when he pulled the back panel off. A long black thing slithered out at his feet. At first glance, it appeared to keep moving, causing Jacob to jump. When he realized it wasn't a snake, and instead was the culprit of all the problems, he let out a sigh. After that, it took another twenty minutes for him to loop the new belt on and stretch it around the pulley. He walked in rather proudly, as Edwin announced, "Mommy, I fixed it."

"Oh, you did, did you?" replied Sylvia, full of pride. "Come here and let's wash those hands and then get you a cookie for fixing it."

Jacob thew the old belt in the kitchen trash, and then asked, "Where's my cookie?"

His question earned him a cockeyed smile from his wife, and a quick kiss followed by a "Thank you."

Jacob went to the dining room and then returned to sit next to his son at the table. Edwin had a chocolate chip cookie in his hands, Jacob had a familiar-looking notebook. This wasn't the book of prayers handed down from generation to generation. This was much newer, but no less significant, and he fully intended on handing this one down as well. It was the map, and at the moment it was incomplete.

"How much area were you able to cover?" Sylvia asked as she took her seat with a cup of coffee.

"Not as much as I would have liked," replied Jacob. He turned the book around and pointed on the map to the area they investigated. Sylvia looked up, surprised, and Jacob fully understood why. He told her they were going to cover from that area all the west to the county line. It was an area he had talked about all week long because of his other experiences in that area. "We had more visitors at the Scar."

"That's what? Twice this month?"

"Yep," answered Jacob. The last time was just three weeks ago. Before that, it had been a month. As he thought back on it, the average was one event with visitors about every two weeks. Still too frequent, and recently it felt like it was growing, but in reality, it wasn't. His tolerance of it was just shorter than before. He always hoped interest would wane, but so far it hadn't. Jacob fully understood the danger of their little secret getting out. It was hard enough to keep the balance when you knew what you were doing. He still debated anyone who thought he knew what he was doing; seriously doubting there were any experts in this at all. What really concerned him was the possible interference by novices or those that don't know any better, coming out and doing something stupid like a seance in the middle of the Scar. To them, it's something interesting they saw on a show or in a movie and wanted to try it, not fully understanding what opening a portal truly meant and why it would be dangerous.

"Did you find what you were looking for, though?" Sylvia asked.

"Surprisingly... no," Jacob said disappointedly.

She grabbed the map again and looked at all the notes Jacob had made over the last several years. Then, with her index finger countered each one before looking back up at Jacob. He knew exactly what her point was. There was a lot of activity in that area. He fully expected to either find an area that felt a little off, or at worst, a few roamers still moving about. If he found that spot, he would have notated it on the map, and then worked to localize the disturbance so he could give the sheriff a more precise location.

"That's a lot of activity for nothing to be there," she remarked, following her count.

"I agree. We only finished about half of it. So, it may still be there. We just haven't found it yet. That is for next weekend, anyway." Jacob pulled the book back and closed it. It was both a physical and a symbolic act. Sylvia fully knew what being married to a Meyer involved, but that didn't mean she was going to accept Jacob's obsessiveness he showed when they first started dating. She understood it, seeing all that had happened, and everything that landed on his shoulders, but it didn't mean she was going to accept it. So, she set ground rules for both of their benefit, or that was at least how she explained it to Jacob. She told him, trying to keep up with all that, the farm and the family was the highway to become a ghost himself. She didn't stop before adding that she wasn't going to be married to a man having an affair with the supernatural. A comment he chuckled about and asked if it would be okay if it was the ghost of Marilyn Monroe. He wore that bruise on his arm for the next few days, and just told people he ran into something in his barn.

Outside of emergency calls, which still came at all hours of the day and night, he had one day a week he could work on things. Other than that, his little side project had to stay in the bag with the cross and his family's book of prayers, and that was his next stop. He placed it in and closed the bag on that work for the week. The bag, though, was never far from his side. He took it everywhere with him.

"Don't forget about dinner with Alice and your father tonight," Sylvia said, regarding the clock that hung on the kitchen wall. It was the same clock that had hung there for longer than his father could remember.

"I won't. Let me go clean up some things out in the barn and I will be right in to get ready."

"Okay, I think I am going to go ahead and bathe Edwin."

The three-year-old that sat next to Jacob turned to him and looked for help. "Uh uh. No bath," he protested.

"Don't look at me, bub. You know your mother is the boss in this house."

Edwin attempted to crawl over Jacob to make a run for it, and Jacob was more than happy to oblige, lifting him up and placing him on the ground. "I'm going to give you a head start, though. Run!" Jacob put him on the ground and Edwin took off. When Sylvia got up to follow, Jacob stood up and embraced his wife. She faked a struggle, but it wasn't much of one.

"This just means you have to give him the next one."

With that revelation, Jacob kissed Sylvia quickly and moved out of her way so she could chase the squealing child. He didn't take part in the chase at all and strolled out to the barn to take care of the aforementioned task.

Halfway out to the barn, he felt a tingle up his back and several pins push into his spine. It was a feeling he had felt so many times; it doesn't even produce the cold sweat it once had. There was no retreat for his bag. No reason to. He normally felt one here. They had a resident on the farm, or make that a partial resident. He wasn't always around, but every few months, he arrived. The regularity of his visits wasn't the most disturbing factor related to this individual. It was what he was, and not just a talker. He knew what he was. He was also aware of where he was and what was going on around him. Supposedly was for years, and completely fine with it. At least that was how he let on.

Jacob slid open the door and looked around quickly, just to be sure. If it was anything else, he could slam the door and start reciting any of the hundreds of prayers he had memorized from the book. When he saw the man in the 1920s flapper attire, he knew it was safe, and entered. "Hey, Reg," Jacob greeted him. Reg didn't know his real name, so Jacob gave him one. Reg wasn't short of Reginald or Reggie. It was Reg, as in short for regular.

He turned from the workbench, where he was studying what Jacob had to imagine was a host of foreign tools and equipment to him. "Hey Jacob. How's the mapping going?"

"Pretty good. We still have a few spots to cover. It would help if you could just tell me where things were."

Reg drifted over to Jacob's trusty tractor. "If I could, I would, but I really don't know anything. Except..." his voice trailed off, and his translucent hand traced the leather wrapped curve of the steering wheel. He had a horrible case of PAHD, Paranormal Attention and Hyperactive Disorder. A condition Jacob created to describe the wondering focus of the spirits he had encountered.

"Except what, Reg?"

"That it didn't hurt to dance with that nice girl."

Jacob took his old ball cap off and slammed it down on the table. He had hoped there was a genuine revelation or something there, not just a smartass reminder from the past. "No, it didn't," Jacob agreed before asking another question. "Reg, is he still out there? We haven't really felt anything in a while. Just the normal spirits here and there."

"Jacob, we've talked about this before," Reg said, focused, leaving the tractor behind. "He is always out there. Don't let yourself be lulled into believing otherwise. That will be when he shows."

It was the same warning he received every time he asked. What was surprising is Father Murray gave him the same warning that a dead guy did. Jacob didn't believe he, or it, was gone, but he didn't have any idea when he would show back up. It could be today, tomorrow, or not in his lifetime. He just didn't know, and no one else did either.

4

Jacob's family invaded Edward and Alice's house early in the evening, and invaded was the right term. The door was barely open before Edwin took off through the crack and into the house, squealing all the way. He was in search of his Papa. Edward had fully embraced being a grandfather, and Edwin had embraced being his grandson.

Alice invited Jacob and Sylvia in while the screams continued from the living room. Edwin had found Edward. After Alice and Edward wed, they moved off of the Meyer's farm, leaving that to Jacob to live in and tend to. Alice had a place in town, just a few blocks away from the city center. Which was convenient. She was a person who often walked through the central square and up and down the line of shops on each side of the row. Not really shopping, but just socializing, and passing the time. For Edward, that was quite a change. He was used to the seclusion of the farm, and while he never really farmed, it wasn't long after he moved in with Alice that he confided in Jacob that he missed the openness and space of the farm. A few years ago, they compromised, and found a place close to downtown, but had enough property to remind Edward of the old farm. Jacob used to joke, it would remind him of it, and learn to hate it the first time he had to mow the yard. Much to his surprise, his father bought a tractor to take care of the chore.

When they rounded the back corner of the hallway and into the living room, where their son now wrestled with Edward, they saw there was an additional guest for dinner who was laughing at the exhibition match occurring in the easy chair in the corner. Father Murray, who stepped down three years ago as the head of their local church after old age robbed him of both the mobility and the energy to tend to his flock, at least how he wanted to do it. He handed the reins over to Father Isaac. He was young, idealistic, and rather wet behind the ears. When Father Murray wasn't out fishing with Lewis, he was helping the new head of his church in the ways of Miller's Crossing. The Vatican told him they fully prepared him before they assigned him, but the squeal he produced the first time he ran into a spirit seemed to tell a different story. It took two days of talking to keep him from leaving the cloth. Father Murray called his Vatican superiors to discuss a replacement after that event. They were understanding, but rejected his request, and reminded the elder priest of his responsibility of counseling. It was a role Father Murray didn't hesitate to take; he just knew the challenges of this place.

"Evening Jacob." Father Murray groaned as he stood up to give Jacob a hug.

"Hi Father."

Then it was Sylvia's turn, and she returned his hug.

"Hey guys," Edward called from underneath Edwin.

"Don't hurt him," Sylvia warned.

"I'll be careful," responded Edward with a laugh.

"She was talking to Edwin dad," chided Jacob.

"Ha ha," laughed Edward.

Jacob walked into the kitchen with Sylvia to see if they could help Alice with anything, and it appeared they had arrived just in time. Everything was ready to be taken to the table. They helped her while Edward entertained Edwin. Once everything was ready, Sylvia went to separate the two children, one much older than the other, and took Edwin to the table. Edward would have to find the table on his own.

These types of family dinners were a regular occurrence for them. Sometimes here. Sometimes at the farm. The day varied, but it was usually on the weekend. Jacob was glad Alice suggested it. With all that had happened to their family, keeping something that appeared normal felt good. He had already lost his mother, and practically lost his sister. This didn't need to be another way to further separate the family, and Alice never treated her marriage to his father that way. Instead, she tried to be an addition to the existing family unit, and Jacob was thankful for that.

In the time he had gotten to know her, he found there were similarities between her and Sylvia, which he had never seen before. Of course, what he remembered of her was her as a teacher. Getting to know the real person was an eye-opening experience. Teachers were real people. Who knew? She laughed, joked, loved, hurt, all sorts of things beyond assigning homework and grading papers. But just like in her classroom, she had rules in her house, and there was one she and Sylvia shared, which Jacob, Edward, and Father Murray broke at the table after dinner.

"Guys, no shop talk at the table," she reminded them with a smile, which Sylvia mirrored as she looked down the table at the three men. It was Edward who broke the rule, and it was Edward who solved the problem, and invited Father Murray and Jacob out to the porch to enjoy an after-dinner beer. On the way out, Jacob heard Sylvia fixing coffee, which was the beverage of choice for the ladies.

"Same thing at my house," Jacob commented as they walked out onto the porch.

"It's a good rule," remarked Father Murray. "Yes, this duty is your family, but it shouldn't interfere with your family."

"That is what I am trying to keep it from doing, Father," Jacob said as he settled into a chair on the porch. "I just have this feeling there is something out there just waiting for us."

"Nothing showing up?"

"Nothing of notice," answered Edward. He took a swig of his beer. Jacob did the same and then looked out at the open field as the night set in above.

"We have found a few things here and there, but nothing even close to what was out there in the Scar. But that's not really worrying me. I didn't expect to find another site like that. I just expected to find something that made sense. Something we could correlate."

"But you have found spots?" Father Murray asked.

"Yes, five," answered Edward.

"Six," corrected Jacob.

"Five and a half," responded Edward. "We disagree on one. If there was anything there, it was very weak."

"Then you have found something." Father Murray settled into his chair and then turned his head to look at Jacob, who was on his right, and then turned again toward Edward, who sat on his left. "I'm not sure I understand then."

"None of the spots we found match any of our past engagements, and the areas we are commonly called out to were just blanks. That part doesn't make sense. They come from some place, especially the more mischievous ones. Where is the question."

"Now Jacob, we talked about this before." Father Murray settled back in his chair and took a swig. "I not only agreed we needed to create a map, but I even said you should do it. I saw that spark in your eye, and knew you would do it right, but you do remember what I cautioned you about, don't you?"

"Yes Father," Jacob sighed.

"What was my caution?"

"You told me not to be so literal and linear in my thinking. That I would be ill advised to apply common sense to the paranormal world."

"That's correct. This isn't like duck hunting where you can find the lake, or fox hunting where you look for the den. We don't know if they come from any specific spot or if the spirits just appear wherever. Any pattern you find could be just random appearances and should not be viewed in any way other than that." Father Murray let that sink in before he asked, "Has the frequency of visits changed any?"

Jacob and Edward regarded each other with an interested look. Inside, Jacob did some quick math, thinking about the last few months. "Not really. Still one or two every week." That had been the pattern since he sealed the portal they believed to be out at the Scar. Whether he had sealed it was a point of contention with his father, and even in that, Jacob was ignoring points of Father Murray's warning. Because the frequency of visits had dropped since that day, he assumed he had. It was linear logic, and only using a small slice of time in the grand scheme of the world.

"Then I say, you keep making the map just in case, noting the areas of interest, and just enjoy the quiet time. This town has been through enough. It deserves to enjoy the quiet, and so do the two of you."

"Now that is something I can toast to." Edward said, and then offered his beer bottle to Father Murray who clinked his against. Father Murray turned and did the same with Jacob. Jacob couldn't agree more.

5

Jacob enjoyed the quiet of the next few days. The lack of any late-night calls allowed him to enjoy being a husband and father. These were periods that neither he nor Sylvia complained about. They were nice snippets of what a normal life was like. Of course, nothing was ever what outsiders would consider normal in Miller's Crossing, and as strange as it sounded, that felt normal to Jacob.

When the phone rang next, it wasn't late at night. It was the middle of the afternoon, but the special ringtone he had assigned to Father Murray, Sheriff Taylor, and Lewis Tillingsly told him everything he needed to know. Sylvia gave him the look she always did. The one begging him to not answer. If he didn't, his father would be next in the call tree. Jacob couldn't do that. This was his responsibility, and he went and grabbed the phone.

"Jacob, can you get down to the Gas and Grub on highway 431?" Sheriff Taylor asked.

"Sure thing. What are we dealing with, sheriff?"

"I'm not sure. Why don't you come join Lewis and me?" he replied rather vaguely.

"On my way." Jacob hung up and grabbed his bag, confused.

"More spirits?" asked Sylvia as Jacob leaned over the sofa to give her a kiss. "Odd for them to be out in the day, isn't it?"

"Not as odd as you think. They are there, but most people don't see them until after nightfall. But this time, I'm not sure. Sheriff Taylor didn't tell me what it was. He just wanted me to join him down on Highway 431."

The confusion Jacob felt continued and led to a great deal of mulling over what could lie ahead of him during the drive. Here in Miller's Crossing, the possibilities were endless, and nothing would surprise him after all he had seen. Sheriff Taylor had never called him without telling him what the problem was. Jacob felt that was out of courtesy, but as he got to know the new sheriff, he realized that was just part of his personality. He was a detailed man. One of those who liked to have a plan, which unsurprisingly was a trait his predecessor possessed too.

As Jacob arrived at the Gas and Grub, he saw two patrol cars pulled into parking places in front of the store. He pulled in next to them and parked. A quick look around found nothing suspicious, but that rarely told Jacob the whole truth. Most of the scenes he pulled up on looked rather normal on the surface. Only when you searched around did you find the truth. Seeing Sheriff Taylor and Deputy Richards inside, Jacob assumed that was where the truth was.

He walked in and noticed both men were standing in the front window, where he saw them from outside. Sheriff Taylor motioned for Jacob to come join them. Jacob did so reluctantly.

"Sheriff, what is it?" Jacob asked. His hand reached inside his bag and clutched the cross.

"Come look at this," Sheriff Taylor responded, and motioned again for him to join them.

Jacob took a few more steps toward them. Sheriff Taylor reached back and grabbed him by the shoulder and pulled him to the window.

"Look across at the motel parking. What do you see?"

Jacob looked through the dirty window of the Gas and Grub and scanned the parking lot for any paranormal guests. Why they were looking from way over here was a complete mystery. They never hesitated to get close to their visitors before. Sheriff Taylor may have acted scared the first few times, but he soon grew used to the frequent visits and interactions. There was nothing. No visitor, and not even what an old 80's movie used to call a free roaming vapor. The lot had probably a dozen cars parked in it, which was pretty busy for a motel on an off the beaten path highway.

"What exactly am I looking for?"

"You don't see it?" Richards asked.

"No." Jacob didn't, and he even took a second look.

"You don't see the big ghost?" asked Sheriff Taylor.

That got Jacob's attention and he all but pressed his face against the glass for a closer look. "Where? I don't see anything."

"See the black hatchback?"

Jacob looked again and located it. "Yep."

"Now look at the van next to it." There was a little laugh after Richards' response.

The white van was hard to miss. It was a large cargo style van with no windows, and about three times the size of the small hatchback it sat next to. Then Jacob saw it. The image that made his heart sink. Painted right there on the side of it was a large purple ghost. Under it in block letters, Paranormal World. Jacob let his head dip.

"I take it you know the show?" asked Sheriff Taylor.

"I'm aware of it," responded Jacob. He didn't make it a habit of watching those kinds of shows for entertainment. They were too close to home, and most of the hosts were over the top. And it sickened Jacob. It made a mockery of what he, his father, and the other keepers dealt with. That didn't stop Sylvia from being a huge fan of those shows when they first started dating. That stopped soon after what she called paranormal hunting became part of her daily life. Paranormal World was one of her favorites. The host, Elmer Daughtry, a slim, graying fellow with an English accent, claimed to be a medium and paranormalist. Even citing some certifications he had received from various official sounding organizations during the opening of the show. Jacob doubted if any of those places even existed beyond a website that would mail you a certificate if you paid the $29.99 fee. "I sure hope he is just passing through."

"If only we were so lucky," remarked Sheriff Taylor. "Tell him what you saw him doing, Andrew."

"He and his camera crew were filming out at the 'Entering Miller's Crossing' sign."

Jacob stepped back from the window and bumped into the rack of chips behind him. "Crap." This was bad. This was really bad. So much for the internet rumors dying down. This guy had the power to give them real and lasting fuel, undoing any gains they may have made through the years. This was a real problem, and there was no script for this. Jacob seriously doubted a cold bath would work here. If anything, it might strengthen all the rumors. "Got any ideas?"

"Not a one. I've already run his tag and performed a search for anything I could use. Both were clean. Not even a trespassing or parking ticket."

"We can't let that guy get anywhere near the Scar. I've seen what he does on the show. Ouija boards, demon worshipping, channeling. If there is anything to him, it would be disastrous. Even if there isn't, that area is so charged, just the presence of those activities might be enough." Jacob felt a chill come over him, and it wasn't from an approaching spirit. He knew the real danger here; the flood of people that would come try their hand at it after seeing that place on his show. That was a fact that existed no matter if Elmer found anything or not. His presence and his show would bring the attention they didn't want or need.

"Tell me something I don't know." Sheriff Taylor turned away from the window. "I'm going to guess we can't reason with him."

Jacob shook his head. That was out of the question. If they even tried to, he would put it all on air, and their secret would be out. This was a problem Jacob had never even considered. They have had bloggers come through, but those don't have a lot of credibility, except with maybe their dozens of followers. The quick cold shower treatment was usually enough to convince them otherwise. This was a journalist. Jacob felt ill even associating him with that word. If he found anything at all interesting, his network might give them a full three hour live prime-time special. If he found the secret, he would be an instant celebrity.

6

"How many people actually watch those shows?" Father Murray asked.

Jacob looked back at his wife, who hid behind her coffee mug. Her wide-star-crossed eyes were visible above its rim.

"A lot."

When Jacob told her what the disturbance was out at the Gas and Grub, she struggled to withhold her enthusiasm. He caught her pulling up a few episodes on a television on-demand service as he walked in and out of the house. Each time, he either gave her an admonishing look or reminded her how dangerous this was.

"Probably just for the humor," commented Father Murray.

"Not quite. There are millions of crack pots out there that watch those shows and believe everything," responded Jacob.

"Jacob, I wouldn't call them crackpots for believing. Remember, they are right."

Jacob nodded at Lewis Tillingsly to agree with the point he just made. To most of the world, those that believed in the existence of ghosts are crackpots. Those that watched those shows were only slightly better. He often wondered what the world would think if they realized it was true.

"So, what do we do about him?" Sheriff Taylor asked. He was nursing his beer in the Meyer's kitchen. The place had served as spook central for decades. Most, if not all, planning on how to deal with the problem that existed at Miller's Crossing occurred here.

"Better question. What do I do about him?"

Every eye in the kitchen shifted to Father Murray, who sat there with a look of dismay.

"His producer called me earlier this afternoon. A gracious woman, Marjorie Tillman, told me they were doing a feature on the internet legend of Miller's Crossing and wondered if I would give them an interview."

"Well, you can't do that," spouted Edward.

"It is completely out of the question," agreed Lewis.

Jacob agreed too, but just nodded. There was nothing more to add, but it appeared Father Murray had something else to say on the topic.

The priest put his coffee back on the table, in its familiar place just in front of where he always sat at the Meyer's kitchen table. The clang it made on its saucer, something Sylvia demanded they used to avoid any further staining of the old table, drew everyone's attention. "I think it's a good idea. I could tell him there is nothing here but old folklore. Nothing more than just ghost stories, handed down from generation to generation."

Jacob was already shaking his head as the Father spoke. When he finished, Jacob moved and leaned next to the large kitchen island across from the table. "You haven't seen his show, have you?"

"Well... no," stumbled Father Murray.

Jacob looked at his wife, who still had those star struck eyes. "You're the resident Elmer expert here. Care to give us a rundown of how the show works?"

She swallowed hard before she started. "I've only seen a few episodes."

"Try a few seasons," Jacob pointed out with a smile. His wife smiled back.

"Okay, I have watched quite a bit of it. In each episode, he introduces where he is. Then there is a montage of scenes to explain what he is there to investigate. He does it up really big and theatric as he tells the story. Then he turns scientific. Talking about the phenomenon involved. After that, he starts his interviews with locals and experts. That is usually the first half of the hour-long episode. The last half..."

"Backup to the interviews," Jacob interrupted. "Tell them about those. I know I noticed a pattern in them, and I'm sure you did, too."

"Oh," she breathed, and the point Jacob hoped she would make seemed to have arrived. "Um, he interviews people who have seen or know others that have seen whatever he is there for, but he also talks to people who haven't and don't believe in it."

"It's his way to be fair and balanced," Jacob walked over and placed his hand on his wife's shoulder, giving it a little rub. She reached up and patted his hand. "You would just be his opposition, and even better, you are a retired priest. They called you because they know you would give them what they need, with the credibility of the church behind it."

This created a collective groan in the room.

"Do we think any locals will actually speak to him?" asked Sheriff Taylor.

"That is what worries me the most. You never know what someone might say in front of a camera with the opportunity of fame sitting in front of them. Imagine if you were the person who helped Elmer find actual proof, and I'm not talking about just unexplained sounds or odd shadows, but actual proof."

"Do you really think he would let anyone but him take credit?" Edward asked.

There was a shared chuckle in the room. They were all thinking about it. Edward was just who said it out loud first.

"True, but that's not what I am thinking about. Elmer may take credit, but you would be the person everyone saw talking about it on his show. Every other show and podcast in the world would want to talk to you," explained Lewis. "That kind of fame, and the money that comes with it, could be rather tempting to some. No matter how committed you are to the cause."

"Then they set up a t-shirt stand. A place for souvenir pictures. Then the bumper stickers—my car got re-possessed in Miller's Crossing. We would be the Area-51 of the paranormal world. Might as well rebuild the bridge over Walter's Creek and rename it the Paranormal Superhighway." Jacob moved before his father slapped him upside the head.

He made the comments in jest, but there was a part of it he feared could become a reality if this got out of hand. At the moment, he didn't see any way it wouldn't. Lewis Tillingsly was right. The allure of the camera can cause people to do funny things. He always regarded their town as an extended family. They all shared the same responsibility and the same secret. One held closely for centuries now. Could the lure of televisions or social media sway one of the younger generation? His mind went to the length he has seen people go to create a viral video. Showing an actual ghost would be one way, but yet, no one has yet. No one has, *yet*. He hoped that was a testament to the community.

"I can spread the word to some of the elders and ask them to talk to their families and the other families they know," Lewis suggested. He removed his wide-brim black hat, the same he wore when he was sheriff and never stopped after his forced second stint in the position, and ran his hand through his white hair. "But there is no way we can talk to everyone."

"I have an idea about that." Father Murray tapped Lewis. "Let me slide out for a moment. I need to make a call." Lewis moved and let the father scoot out. Father Murray walked toward the backdoor, but stopped short, and pulled out his cell phone. He turned to the others and motioned with his hands for the others to continue talking. When they didn't, he turned and chastised them. "This is my idea. Y'all need to find a way to get rid of this nuisance."

"Did Father Murray just say y'all?" asked Sylvia. She elongated the word in her poor attempt at a southern accent. She giggled. The others didn't. They were straining to hear what Father Murray was saying.

"Todd," Father Murray said to the person on the other end of the call. From that, they all knew he was talking to Father Todd Isaac. "We have a little situation going on here. I can provide more information later, but I need you to make your sermon this Sunday and the topic at prayer meeting tomorrow all about temptation, and the sins that can come with it. Can you do that?"

There was a pause, and everyone listened closely to hear what the response would be.

"Good. Good," Father Murray said, and then paused again. "You know I don't like meddling in how you run the church now. It is your church, but this is something different, and I will explain when I see you. Thanks Todd."

He hung up and turned back to the kitchen full of friends, regarding them with a humorous look. "Bunch of nosey nellies. That's handled, how about your problem?" He asked as he reached across the table for his coffee cup, and then went to pour himself another cup.

"Not yet," Edward said with a wipe of his forehead.

"That's a dumb idea," muttered Sylvia, and she pushed away from the table and went to join Father Murray in pouring another cup of coffee.

"What's a dumb idea?" asked Jacob. He followed his wife to the counter where the coffeemaker was. "Darling, what's the idea?"

"Just some stupid Scooby Doo sounding scheme." She said and turned back to the room with a fresh cup of coffee, which she promptly took a sip from. Five sets of eager eyes met her. Not a one of them had any ideas themselves. "Why not give him what he wants? In a way of speaking?"

The eager looks changed to ones of complete disbelief, with a few shaking their heads.

"I don't mean really let him get out there and find the real thing. I am saying, show him something like what we see on the show. Some unexplained noises. A shadow or two. Divert him from the truth by feeding him what he wants. He has seen and sold so much of the fake stuff; I doubt he would really recognize anything real. He would be satisfied and leave, thinking he has a great show. His viewers will see more of the same, love it because they love his shows, but that is it. It won't really entice anyone to rush down here and see anything for themselves."

When how genius the idea was finally sunk in on Jacob, he leaned in and gave his wife a kiss, which she readily accepted. There seemed to be some acceptance of the concept around the room. There were still lots of challenges to it. Jacob knew that. But they had spent years performing a ruse to deal with visitors. Why not another one this time?

"If this is going to work, we need to elicit help," Jacob said. "We will need people that are in on it to feed him stories, and others to tell him those people are crazy."

"We can make it about the old factory out on Pickering. It is the complete opposite side of town from the Scar," stated Lewis.

"In the meantime, I will double the patrols out at Scar, and maybe add a few more signs about the toxic chemicals on the property for good measure."

"Good idea, sheriff," said Edward. Jacob saw an expression of enthusiasm on his father's face. He appeared to be completely onboard with the idea. "That will help if they drive around exploring. I know most of the online rumors are about the Scar, but we can even explain that its appearance draws that attention and explain it's really an area that suffered a horrible chemical spill, stressing the danger to him and his crew if they go there."

"It might work," Jacob said, still rolling the details around in his head. "It will disappoint him, since the tales about the Scar are probably what brought him here, but we can point out how those were wrong, and how many others have made those mistakes and had to be hospitalized because of exposure to the toxic chemicals." Jacob turned to Sheriff Taylor. "We keep records of everyone who we decontaminate, right?"

"Yes, but if you are thinking about providing them to him, I need to remind you about medical privacy."

"I know," Jacob said, and he did. "We can redact the names. I am just thinking the records might help solidify our story. Remember, this is why we asked the hospital to treat them like an actual patient."

The plan was taking shape, and Jacob was feeling more comfortable with it by the moment. But not completely comfortable. This was still shaky and, as Sylvia put it, a Scooby-Doo plan. All they needed to do at the end was have Elmer pull the mask off old Mr. Henderson, who was trying to scare people from his farm. This was the only plan they had. The only other alternative was to tell Elmer Daughtry to go away, but Jacob wasn't stupid. He knew that would have the opposite reaction, make him more obsessed with finding the truth. This was it. It had to be.

7

"So, this is the fellowship of the crossing?" cracked Edward as he walked into the church. This wasn't the first time Jacob and his father had gathered here at such a late hour. Back when Father Murray was the head of their local church, it was rather commonplace. Now that Father Isaac was there, it didn't happen as much. It's not that he didn't get involved in the events in the crossing. He did, reluctantly. Gone are the days when the head of the church took the lead. Father Murray still tried to do so when he could. The years had taken their toll on him. Arthritis slowed his movement, and a nasty cough brought on by any cooler weather put him out of commission all together.

"All right, who is playing good cop and who is playing bad cop?" Lewis asked.

"Depends on what you consider good and what is bad. I think I can handle the lying. God knows there is a bit of that in gossip." Ruthie Day raised her hand. A tower of unnaturally red hair extended almost a foot high above her head.

"That's perfect," said Sylvia. "In small towns, Elmer Daughtry considers places like beauty salons and bars as information centers. He performs his interviews of locals there."

"So, Ruthie, which lie would you be telling?" asked Fred Ralph. He sat two pews away, holding his hunting cap in his hand. "The one where the factory is where all the spooks are, or the one where there is nothing at all around here?"

"I'll tell the one about the factory. You are crotchety enough looking to be the old guy in town who thinks everyone is nuts," Ruthie said with a smile.

"That's good. That plays right in to how the show goes."

"Thanks, I guess," Fred sarcastically conceded. The smile was not a proud one. It was part of the ongoing war that happened across the main street between Ruthie and Fred. The opening salvos occurred every day while they each swept off the sidewalk in front of their stores. It was a friendly war. The weapons of choice, sarcasm and insults that brought smiles to each of their faces. Neither of them would have it any other way.

"Ruthie, can you get the others to join in?" Sylvia asked. Jacob smiled to himself as he realized his wife had now taken over the position of ringleader in this scheme. Of course, it was her scheme, so why shouldn't she? She was also the town's self-declared Elmer Daughtry expert.

"Piece of cake," Ruthie responded with a flip of her hand, to wave off what she obviously felt was an annoying question. Jacob didn't doubt that Ruthie could get the rest of her court to join in there are the salon. She was their queen, after all.

What Jacob still doubted was this plan. He paced up at the front of the church. All the things that could go wrong here played in his head as warnings of all the reasons they shouldn't do this. What kept pushing back against them was the drought where alternatives were concerned. There were none, besides let Elmer Daughtry do what he does, and just what? Pray for the best?

That was a horrible option, and Jacob knew it. He and Sheriff Taylor had texted all night last night about trumping up some traffic charge or ticketing him for trespassing if he tried to go to the Scar. Both would force him to leave. But both would just cause more attention. One of those Hollywood tabloid shows would pick up the story if they pulled him over and detained him, and trespassing him from the Scar would just feed the internet rumors even more. Jacob fully felt they were in a damned if they do, damned if they don't situation, and he didn't like it.

"Sylvia, how deep should I lay it on?"

"As deep as you can, Ruthie. Go over the top. That will guarantee you to make the cut."

"Alice and I checked out a few of his shows last night. It looks like he finds all the local crazies to put on the show. Most claim to have seen the ghosts he was there to investigate. A lot claim it had possessed or haunted them. Kind of like those on the UFO shows that claimed to have been abducted," Edward said.

Fred laughed, a deep chuckle that echoed up in the rafters of the church, and then slapped his knee with the hunting cap. "Crazies. They picked the right one there."

"Oh, you old fool, he was talking about you, too. You are going to be on there with me."

Fred's laugh stopped as that fact settled in, but the rest of those in the church snickered. Some tried to hide it. If they wanted the town crazies, Jacob knew they picked the right two. These were the two with the biggest personalities in town, and if anyone ever asked who to talk to about anything, they would point to them, or Father Murray and the Meyers, who would push them in their direction.

Father Murray stood up, pushing against the back of the pew to steady himself. "Okay, we have our players, so what's the play?"

"I just tell him there are nothing but stories, and fools that believe in it," responded Ralph. He looked around for confirmation if he had it right, and he did.

"You will just need to elaborate on it a bit more, but you're right," confirmed Sylvia.

"Roger. Stretch it out. I can do that. Maybe throw in some stories about teens that take people out there as a prank, or a hazing for the local high school."

"That's perfect, Mr. Ralph."

He sat back in the pew and smiled smugly at Ruthie Day.

"I'm not much worried about your story, Fred. It's Ruthie's," said Father Murray.

"The Father is right," started Sylvia. "Your story needs to be deep and has to have some kind of backstory. Like an urban legend. He will then want to do some research into that story."

"Well, how detailed?" asked Ruthie. She seemed concerned now. Her flamboyant confidence drained away.

"Really detailed," Sylvia said as she sat down on her knees in the pew in front of Ruthie. "It needs to be really detailed. For example, he visited an old reform school up in Evanston in one of his first seasons. The story was every night you could hear the screams of the tortured children who died there. He talked to people who braved it themselves and told him their story of what they saw and heard. The town expert, which would be you Ruthie, told him of a student who died during a punishment in the room in the south hall back in 1923 or 24. I can't really remember." Sylvia turned and looked around at everyone else, especially her husband. Jacob saw the look on her face. It was almost fearful.

"It needs to really be believable. He will ask around and look up things in town records. In that episode, he found the death certificates of the students."

Now Jacob understood, and he turned to his father and Sheriff Taylor. "Can we do that?" he asked, not wanting to ask the sheriff out loud if they could forge documents to back up this fictional story. There was a shared moment of silence as everyone appeared deep in thought. Jacob was working through all the layers of information they would need to forge to make it lock tight. It seemed unsurmountable. He hadn't really seen too many of Elmer's shows, but he had seen others that were similar, but more of the crime solving variety. Every one of them goes to the library to check old newspapers.

"Father? Do you remember any old stories from the town's past we can use?" asked Sheriff Taylor.

Father Murray thought for a moment before shaking his head and answering, "No." His voice shook, as did many of those in the room. They had hit a roadblock, and the related silence was deafening.

Of all people to save the day, Ruthie Day spoke up and broke the silence. "Lewis, Ned Winter's daughter. What year was that?"

Lewis responded instantly. The mountain top might have some snow on it, but the fire within still raged. He was as sharp as a tack when it came to remembering old cases, and people from Miller's Crossing. "Sixty-seven. What'cha thinking, Ruthie?"

That was the question everyone had on their mind. Jacob stopped pacing and sat down on the first pew and looked back at Ruthie in the third pew back. Sylvia was in the second. From there, Jacob could smell his wife's perfume, and felt the need to reach over and grab her hand.

"That crash was out that way. If I remember, it was right in front of the old mill. We could use that as the story. Say it was a violent crash, and her spirit roams that road and the adjacent mill. There are lots of stories like that everywhere, and if he does any research, he will find everything he needs." The room felt renewed, even if it was just slightly. "And better yet, there are no living relatives left to get upset by us using that story."

Over the next hour, Jacob and the others worked out the details of the story they were going to feed Elmer Daughtry. Each detail they clarified for Ruthie gave Jacob more confidence in the plan and energized the room. They were buzzing back and forth, building the story, and listening to Ruthie rehearse how she and the rest of her court would deliver it. Each time, they gave little critiques. Most were asking her to add something of grandeur to it. An odd request to a woman as flamboyant as she was. There were very few requests to bring it back to earth.

Once they were happy with it, sometime around two in the morning, Sylvia asked a question no one had considered. "Now, how do we spring the trap?"

Everyone, including her husband, looked at her, puzzled.

"We have to make sure he talks to Ruthie and Mr. Ralph."

8

"So, this is how you used to do it?" Jacob asked from the back seat of Sheriff Taylor's cruiser. His father sat next to him, and Lewis Tillingsly was in the front seat. He chuckled at the question.

"Yep. There were a ton of stakeouts in the crime ridden town we have here."

The three men were watching Sheriff Taylor walk up and down the sidewalk of Main Street, greeting and conversing with everyone, as he often did. Sometimes at night, working as an old-fashioned doorknocker. Walking up one side and down the other side, checking each of the shop doors to make sure things were locked up tight. Miller's Crossing was a small town, but that didn't mean there wasn't the opportunity of crime. Usually just mischievous teens, sometimes from a neighboring town. Today was a more purposeful patrol. Fred Ralph saw Elmer Daughtry and his production crew going into Len's for breakfast. This presented a perfect opportunity to, as Sylvia put it last night, spring their trap and it was up to the sheriff to do it. Jacob just hoped he wasn't too obvious about it. He noticed he seemed to stand in front of Len's for an unnatural length of time, with his hands on his belt. Just like many a television sheriff.

"Here we go," Lewis called out once the first of the production crew came out of Len's door. Their t-shirts with Elmer's logo on them gave them away. Sheriff Taylor took notice, but only glanced over his shoulder every once in a while, while he rocked back and forth on his feet.

"And contact."

There he was. Elmer Daughtry. Jacob noticed how he looked just as he did on the show. Brown tweed jacket with his signature underneath. There was no Paranormal World t-shirt for him. Either this man thought the camera was always on, or they were going to be turning the camera on shortly. Sheriff Taylor turned and introduced himself. The two men shook hands.

"Let it sit there for a minute, rookie," instructed Lewis from the front seat. There was no way for Sheriff Taylor to hear or for them to hear what he and Elmer talked about.

"Now set the hook."

Jacob chuckled when he realized what Lewis Tillingsly was doing. Elmer was the big fish, and Sheriff Taylor was out there fishing.

When the sheriff turned to point out Ruthie's and Ralph's, Lewis said, "Reel him in."

Elmer looked at the town and then he himself pointed at the two storefronts Sheriff Taylor pointed out to him moments ago. The look on his face was a man that was interested, but Jacob knew they had him when he called over several members of his crew and they talked with the sheriff a few minutes before disbursing and heading toward Ruthie's.

"He landed it."

The three men sat and watched as Sheriff Taylor walked back to the cruiser, grinning from ear to ear. The door creaked as he opened it and got in.

"Nice job rookie." Lewis slapped him on the shoulder. "Did he take the bait? Hook, line, and sinker?" Lewis looked back at Edward and Jacob. Jacob could only shake his head and wonder if there were going to be any more fishing references.

"He sure did. His producer is over talking to Ruthie now."

"That was maybe a bit too easy," commented Edward.

Jacob had to agree with his father. This was too easy, but it was the easiest part. It played right into what Elmer needed for his show. The next step was the hardest of the entire plan. Delivering a convincing enough story to make Elmer forget all the posted urban legends and stories about this place.

"I agree," said Sheriff Taylor. "That's why I bought some insurance policies." He turned around to look at the two men in the back seat. Edward and Jacob shared a confused look. "I've deputized you two."

The objections from Jacob and his father were quick and hardy, but Sheriff Taylor wasn't having any of it.

"Now. Now. He mentioned needing a guide around town. So, being the sheriff, I want to look out for our visitors and make sure no one interferes with their show. What better way than to offer up two deputies to escort him and his crew around for the two days they are here?"

Jacob felt sick to his stomach. He knew the sheriff was right, he just didn't want him to be.

"I like the idea," Lewis Tillingsly commented with a smile. Two very evil looks meet his agreement with the idea. He turned back to the front of the cruiser sheepishly.

"Look. This way, we can stay close and make sure everything is going according to plan."

Jacob knew that was where he was going with his suggestion, and it made sense. It made a lot of sense. So much so, neither he nor his father could offer any sort of real argument beyond just the objection of not wanting to do it. The plan they had was shaky at best. This was, as Sheriff Taylor called it, "an insurance policy." He had accepted the idea, and even looked forward to it when Sheriff Taylor announced, "Now we need to get you guys suited up."

The four men drove back to the Miller's Crossing Police Department. Edward and Jacob waited out in the waiting area while Lewis and Sheriff Taylor went to the back. When they called the Meyers back, they directed each to an individual office. Jacob heard the door close behind him and then heard his father's groan from the other side of the wall. A quick look around the room explained where that groan had come from, and Jacob let out one of his own. He stared at the uniform for a few moments before conceding it was necessary and went to putting it on.

When he walked out, his father was already out there being checked and straightened up by Lewis. Simple things like how he tucked in his shirt or that the belt went through the buckle and around and tucked back under the first clip to help support the weight of the flashlight. Then it was Jacob's turn for an inspection. He hadn't made the same mistakes his father had. Not because he knew better. It was just dumb luck.

"Well, I must say. You two make fine looking deputies. I would have been proud to have you on my force." Lewis threw an arm around each of them. He was enjoying this too much, and Jacob wondered how fast he could get him in cuffs.

They drove back toward Main Street, but parked a few blocks away, walking the rest of the way on foot to make it appear they were on some kind of foot patrol. Jacob hoped they didn't pass anyone at all. Forget worrying about passing anyone he knew. They knew everyone. But, even if they passed or saw anyone from a distance, it was going to be a problem, whether or not they recognized them. Their presence had now doubled the size of the Miller's Crossing police department, and there wasn't a chance that would go unnoticed.

On Main Street, they found Elmer and his crew filming B-roll scenes, which were just random clips of the small town, just like he told Sheriff Taylor they would be. The three officers walked over to the tall, slim, gray-haired man. Lewis parked his butt on a bench outside of Ruthie's.

They watched in silence as the crew did their job. Over the next few minutes, they took segments. Nothing was more than a minute or two. Some of just the road. Some of the sidewalk on one side of the road, and then the other. It was a rushed job to catch a car coming down the road, which was the only traffic while they were there. The crew broke down the tripods and equipment after a brief conversation between Elmer and a blonde in glasses. He assumed she was his producer. She was the one directing everyone during their random shots.

Elmer walked over to the three of them while his crew took most of the equipment to their van. "So, sheriff, are these my escorts to keep the good people of this town from causing an issue?"

Before now, Jacob was sure the English accent he heard on the show was fake, but if it was, it was a long practiced and learned one. It sounded more natural in person.

"Yes sir. They are two of my finest. Both were born and raised here, so they are very familiar with the town. This is deputy Meyer," he pointed to Jacob, "and this is deputy Miller." He pointed to Jacob's father. Jacob wondered who would be the first to forget who was who.

"Well, that is simply fine. Local knowledge is a requirement for a good show. Much gratitude to you, sheriff." Elmer reached forward to shake both Jacob's and Edward's hands, but there was no introduction, as if he expected everyone would know who he was. "Now, we are only here through tomorrow, so time is of the essence. We need to do the interviews this morning, and then set up for our investigation tonight."

"Completely understood," said Sheriff Taylor. "Where would you like to start?"

Elmer looked back at who Jacob assumed was his producer.

"The hairdresser," she said, dropping the r's from each word.

"Ruthie Day," translated Elmer.

"That's fine. Deputy Meyer, will you escort our guest down to Ruthie's?"

"Yes, sheriff," responded Jacob, and he stepped through the group and up the sidewalk, but no one followed.

"Just a minute. I need to get ready."

And there it was. That was the moment Hollywood showed up. The man that had been standing there talking to them retreated to his van, where there was a rollout makeup cabinet and mirror. It took the better part of a quarter of an hour for him to apply powder to remove the color from his face, and then add all sorts of other cremes to add it back, almost to where he looked like a clown. Sylvia never took that much time to get ready, thought Jacob.

After the clown was ready, Jacob led him and his crew of five with their cameras and microphones up the sidewalk to Ruthie's. Jacob held the door open and let him walk in first, then followed by his crew. They all moved to the side, leaving Elmer standing in the center of the entry. It was only when Jacob entered did he step aside.

"Deputy Meyer, care to introduce me?"

Every jaw in the place dropped.

9

"Folks, I understand the reaction," announced Elmer. "I'm just a normal person here to talk to you about your little legend here." He turned back to Jacob. "I guess there is no need for introductions."

Jacob moved by Elmer and slipped through Ruthie's court of friends that always gathered at the salon. Eyes followed him, and not Elmer, as did what sounded like snickers. When he reached where Sylvia was standing, leaning against a stool, she leaned forward and whispered. "Nice uniform." Then Jacob felt a little pat on his butt. He cringed, knowing it was going to be a while before he lived this down, but he knew he needed to put that aside and do his job here. He weaved through the crowd to the back, where Ruthie sat in a salon chair he never saw anyone sitting in for an actual hair appointment.

"Mr. Daughtry, this is Ruthie Day."

Jacob motioned toward Ruthie, who, from the looks of it, was ready for her close-up. Her hair was rivaling the tallest trees in the crossing, and her makeup was applied, though not expertly. This probably could be a great commercial for her shop, but that wasn't his worry. His worry was Ruthie's performance. Especially after the text messages back and forth with Sylvia throughout the night to remind her, and everyone in the group text, that she was the lead in the school play all three years of high school. Shakespeare in the Park, it was not, but it didn't need to be. It just needed to be convincing.

"Back here is perfect." Elmer looked around and then pointed. "Set up over there, and we will do it from this angle." Then he turned his attention to Ruthie. "Mrs. Day, my name is Elmer Daughtry. I host a show called Paranormal World, where we investigate ghost sightings and urban legends. I hear there is a legend here, and Sheriff Taylor said you would be someone I should talk to about it."

"Why sure," she said, over pronouncing each word. Now Jacob was worried.

The blonde in the glasses rushed around behind them, setting up the camera and microphones. Then she squeezed through between Jacob and Elmer and, without asking, clipped a microphone to the collar of Ruthie's floral blouse.

"Should I sit, or should I stand?" Ruthie attempted to ask her, but the woman paid her no attention. She just sped away to recheck the camera.

"Why don't you sit right there?" suggested Elmer. He pointed back at the chair she sat in when they entered. He looked back behind him at his crew and once they all stopped moving, he asked, "Ready?"

They only nodded, and then the lights went on.

So did Ruthie's. Her eyes shot wide open, and Jacob watched intensely to make sure the overweight woman was breathing. It took a bit, but she finally inhaled.

"Ruthie Day, tell me about the mystery of the Old Mill out on Pickering, or what the legend calls the Scar."

Ruthie, to her credit, didn't even wince at hearing that name. She went right into her script, which they all worked out carefully the night before. "Well, I can tell you about the Old Mill, but I'm afraid there isn't much to tell about the Scar except a bad environmental nightmare."

Elmer appeared surprised, but the camera would never show that. He wasn't in the shot. This shot was all about Ruthie. "Can you explain? There are rumors and legends all over the internet about the Scar."

"Oh, we know. Trust me, we all know, and we're not surprised. That place looks like the perfect scene for any Hollywood disaster movie. Nothing but downed trees, and desolate ground, and a crashed tanker that is sitting there rusting because no one will take responsibility for the cleanup, but I can tell you that place is dangerous. No one from Miller's Crossing will even go near it. The hydrochloric acid that spilled when the tanker crashed ruined that ground. Nothing will grow there, and if you are stupid enough to step foot out there, your skin will eventually begin burning. If you don't believe me, ask all those stupid kids that believe what they say online and come out to check for themselves. Each of them ends up in the hospital having to be washed in a cold-water decontamination shower."

Elmer turned around to look at Jacob. "We can edit this out," he remarked and then asked, "Deputy Meyer, is that true?"

"It is. We have the crash report, and years of hospital records we can produce, patient name's redacted, of course. A few come every month to follow the legend and learn a painful lesson." Jacob hooked his thumbs through his belt loop to channel his inner Sheriff Taylor.

Elmer looked away, lost in thought. Then he turned to his crew, after a rather lengthy, awkward silence. "We'll avoid that place." Then he turned back to Ruthie. "The internet is an awesome source of information, but also a source of misinformation. It would appear, in this instance, it is the latter. So, let's talk about the Old Mill. I believe that legend and that other location has been merged by those that don't really know the truth. Let us clear that misconception and shine a light on the truth. So, the old mill?"

Jacob breathed a sigh of relief. He thought he heard others in the room do the same.

"The Davis Saw Mill was the largest single employer in Miller's Crossing until the early 60's when larger mills began winning all the major supplier bids, and also buying up all the land. Which meant at first, they couldn't sell what they had, and then nothing was coming in. It's been empty ever since and became the source of ghost stories among the local teens, which at the time I was one. Then, in 1967, there was a horrible crash out that way. A teenage girl. A friend of mine.... Do I need to tell you her name?"

"If you could?" responded Elmer. "We can look up the details to collaborate it, but will leave the specifics out of the show."

"Sharon Winter. She went into a tree off the northbound side of Pickering. No one knows why she veered off the road and into the trees. They checked the car. There were no defects beyond the crash damage. And there was no one else out there. She was late coming home from a friend's house, and her father called the Sheriff's office. It took a while, but late that night they found her car deep in the woods, where it went head on into a tree. Ever since then, teens and others reported seeing a ghostly figure crossing the road where the accident happened. Now, if you ask me," Ruthie leaned forward and was in her I'm-about-to-spread-gossip pose. "There are two ways to look at it. That is either her, or—and this is what I believe—that ghost walking across the road is what she saw, and she swerved, thinking she was about to hit someone."

"Interesting. Have you ever seen that ghost yourself?"

"Oh no, and I'm too much of a scaredy-cat to ever venture out that way, but many others have." Right on cue, Ruthie looked around Elmer to her court. Half of which raised their hands.

Elmer followed her gaze and then smiled at the sight. "So, each of you have seen it?"

They all nodded, and the smile on Elmer's face grew.

"What I have heard is it continues across and into the mill. Some have followed it, and they say it isn't alone."

Ruthie laid that last bit on deep, but Elmer didn't care. He was now in a room full of eyewitnesses.

"Have any of you followed it into the mill?"

All the hands except one fell. It was now time for our supporting actress to take the stage. Jacob only hoped she didn't become star struck.

Elmer moved through the court, pulling a spare chair with him. He placed it right in front of the person with her hand still raised. Sylvia Meyer. She slowly lowered it back down onto her lap and looked at him. She appeared slightly afraid.

"So, child," he said, regarding her. Sylvia had made herself up to look younger than she really was. It was all her idea. She wanted to appear young enough to be one of those impulsive teens that would sneak out at night and go out to some place like the mill just to check it all out for herself. Jacob tried to convince her she could easily say it was something she did when she was a teen, but she felt compelled to become a teen. "Did you follow the ghosts?"

The man operating the camera swung around to focus on Sylvia. Jacob had a feeling this was the reason she was so eager to play a bit part in this scheme. She loved the show. Now she was on it.

"Yes," she said. Nerves shook her voice.

Jacob thought—Oh no.

Elmer appeared to notice as well. "It's all right, honey. There is no reason to be nervous. Just talk to me like I am a normal person."

The pretentiousness of the man got to Jacob, but he couldn't say anything. All he could do was sit there and watch his wife flounder in a moment she talked about all night long. "Oh, it's not that. Just thinking back to that... I don't know. It just bothers me. Scares me."

Jacob had to turn to hide his smile. His wife had just suckered them both in.

"Well, tell me all about it," prompted Elmer. He moved even closer to his number one fan.

Sylvia swallowed hard and then gave the best performance of all time. "Me and some friends wanted to see if the legend was true. So, we rode out there and sat right at the spot, and waited. At first, there was nothing. Tommy started making jokes and saying we were all fools for believing it. He wanted to leave, but the rest of us convinced him to stay for a little while longer. That was when she walked across the road, right through our headlights. A girl with long, flowing hair. Just thinking about how we could see through her." Sylvia pulled her arms tight and shivered. "We sat there and watched her walk toward the mill, and at first didn't follow. But when she disappeared through the front entrance, we got out and followed through the gate and in through the open delivery door."

She paused and rubbed her eyes. "Inside was a nightmare. There were sounds and voices coming from everywhere. Sounds of footsteps, doors opening, things falling. We didn't make it more than a few feet inside, and then a hard breeze pushed back through the door while something wailed, 'Get Out'. That was it. We all ran back to the car and pulled off as fast as we could. I laid in the back seat and shook. I didn't want to look up. I was afraid of what was following us."

Sylvia sold it, and Elmer bought it. He stood up, slapping his hands together. Jacob worried it might have been too good. Now they needed to figure out how to create a scene to match what she described, and fast.

"That was perfect, young lady. Simply perfect." He looked back at the camera and slashed across his throat. The red light on the front and the bright light attached to the top both shut off. "Deputy, I think we have everything we need here."

10

"So where is this Fred Ralph fellow?"

"This way." Jacob directed Elmer Daughtry across the street to Fred's store. Sheriff Taylor and Edward were standing by the front door, waiting for them. Elmer walked by both of them without even a hesitation and opened the door himself.

"Sheriff, can I talk to you for a minute?" Jacob said and then grabbed Sheriff Taylor by the arm. Edward followed Elmer and his crew inside.

"How'd it go?"

"It went perfect. Ruthie and Sylvia did what they needed to do, but I'm afraid my wife went a little off script and described a real horrifying scene."

"That's great," responded Sheriff Taylor.

Jacob shook his head. "You're not understanding. She really painted quite the scene. I'm not sure we can come close."

"Oh. Oh!" Sheriff Taylor got it, and he pulled his cell phone from his pocket and punched in a number.

"Lewis, the plan is going great, but can you get over to Ruthie's and talk to Sylvia and find out exactly what she described?" There was a pause and some head nodding that Lewis Tillingsly would never see. "Yep, and then if you and the Father can try to get started, that would be great. We will join you as soon as we can, and recruit as many as you need." He hung up. "How good of a picture did she paint?"

"Basically, every paranormal horror movie rolled into one."

The sheriff rolled his eyes and then reached for the door handle. When they walked in, the production crew was busy setting up. Elmer and Fred were talking up a storm. Fred was giving him the history of his store, the first such store in Miller's Crossing, as he told everyone that would listen. The two sat on stools at the soda counter. The old signs behind it on the wall screamed small town from the 1950's, which Jacob felt was perfect. That was the image they were trying to portray.

Both lights on the camera went on, and Elmer took control of the history lesson. "Fred, this is just an informal conversation. I want you to tell me what you know about the Old Mill and the purported ghost that inhabit it."

"There is nothing there besides a family's tragedy and a bunch of overactive imaginations," started Fred. "And I am being serious. Back in the fall of 1967, a young girl died in a crash out that way. I remember her father, Ned. It broke him up something horrible. He was never the same after that. Then he had to survive the daily reminder of it from some stupid ghost story that either his daughter was out there walking around, or some ghost walking across the road caused her to crash in the trees. It plum drove him crazy toward the end of his days. He would go out there and sit waiting for his daughter to come walking by."

"Do you know if he ever saw her?"

"I'm sure of it."

Elmer leaned forward in his chair and his eyes twinkles. Jacob's stomach flopped.

"I'm sure he saw here," continued Fred. "I'm sure she was waiting to embrace and welcome him the day he died in 2003. It's all stupid. I know they didn't find anything wrong with her car, but there are many explanations for what happened."

"Like?" asked Elmer, the twinkle now gone.

"Speed. Fog making the curve hard to see. An animal running across the road. All plausible causes of a crash."

"True, they are all perfectly reasonable causes for a crash, but there could be others."

Fred leaned back against the counter and folded his arms. "I don't want to speak ill about the dead, but maybe she was a careless driver."

Elmer leaned back and mimicked Fred's posture. Arms crossed and all. "I am talking about that of the supernatural variety. Have you ever been out that way?"

"I have," responded Fred shortly.

"And have you seen or heard anything?"

"Not a thing. It's just an empty road beside an old closed down mill that is the place for bored teenagers to go to and get into trouble."

Elmer seemed undeterred by hearing Fred's opinion. "Tell me, Fred. I just talked to a young woman that told me a chilling tale of sounds and creatures out there. Have you ever been to the mill?"

"I have. Several times. Once, even with our former sheriff to shoo away some kids."

"Did you hear or observe anything while out there?"

"Of course I did," answered Fred.

Jacob's heart sank again. Did Fred just blow it for them? While they scripted Ruthie's and Sylvia's parts, they couldn't do the same for Fred. This segment aways do more of a question-and-answer style. Any scripting would only get them so far. The rest would be up to Fred.

"It's a noisy place out there. It's an old mill. Lots of equipment and machinery out there. Large metal doors. Even a slight breeze will bring that place alive. Doors moving, equipment rattling. Plus, being abandoned like it is, you know there is wildlife using it as a home."

"Possibly," said Elmer. This is right in line with the episodes Jacob had seen. He never challenged either side.

"It's a fact," Fred leaned in. "Add in the imagination of a teenager, and one that might have been taking some nips from their parent's liquor cabinet or just finished off a six-pack with some friends, and there you have it."

"I have one last question for you, Fred. Do you believe in the paranormal?"

The store was silent before, and now it seemed even more so. This was a question. If you asked anyone in Miller's Crossing, you would get a resounding yes.

"You mean ghosts?" countered Fred.

"Ghosts. Spirits. Demons. Do you believe in those, Fred?"

Fred glanced at Edward and Jacob and then stared right into Elmer's eyes. "I believe in what I can see." He smiled after his answer.

Elmer reached forward and shook Fred's hand. "Thank you, Mr. Ralph. That was simply perfect."

"Glad to help. Do we need to re-cut anything? Is the lighting okay in here? It's an old store."

Without checking with his producer, Elmer answered, "No. I think everything was fine." He shook Fred's hand again and then headed for the door.

Fred winked at Jacob and Edward. Then the sheriff and his two deputies followed Elmer out of the old store, letting Fred get back to business, which really was light this morning. There was a crowd outside watching, but it was mostly Ruthie's court, which had crossed enemy lines to come watch the event through the store's front window.

"Why don't you guys go in there and get something to drink? Standing out here with your faces plastered to the glass probably makes you all awfully thirsty," commented Jacob, channeling his inner authority figure. Several of them took his suggestion and headed in. Sylvia was one of them. He knew she was curious how Fred did and was most likely in there to get a full report.

"Sheriff," started Elmer. He turned before he reached the curb. "These interviews were perfect. I can't thank you and your deputies enough for being so accommodating. Many places we go, they treat us as more of a nuisance."

"Our pleasure," replied the sheriff, again with his thumbs looped through his belt buckles. "We are here to help. In fact, we would like to help you out around the mill. Setup a perimeter to keep out any lookie-loos. We don't have many celebrities come through town. After your interviews with Ruthie and Fred, word of your presence is bound to spread."

"That would be wonderful. We will be out there around 10pm setting up and will start our investigation around midnight. That is when most areas become active."

Jacob didn't want to tell him time had nothing to do with when things were active around here, but that was a side they didn't want Elmer to see. A quick check of his phone told him they had just over twelve hours to set up the side of Miller's Crossing they wanted him to see.

11

"Are you sure this is going to work?"

Sylvia answered with a shrug.

Jacob looked at Father Murray for an answer to his question. He hoped to find one more definitive than what he received from his wife, but not all hopes come true. It was just another shrug, which sent Jacob into a stress induced pace. He was out there with his wife, several of their friends, and Father Murray to oversee what Lewis Tillingsly called Operation Spook.

The younger members of the operation had a little more experience at this than Father Murray had. They set up the Miller's Crossing haunted house each of the last seven years. They, make it Sylvia, recruited Jacob five years ago as an expert in the matter. Father Murray checked things, and then left, commenting that running around an old mill was a young person's game. Sheriff Taylor and Deputy Edward Miller setup roadblocks to provide Elmer Daughtry and his crew a pristine environment for his investigation.

"It will work," Charlotte said, but she didn't sound too convinced.

Jacob ran through it again in his mind. It would sit quietly until they saw Elmer and his team approach the mill. Then slowly, they would release one trick at a time. Each would be a long way away from them. That was Jacob's doing. The distance helped mask how fake certain things would sound. Each person would be positioned deep in the mill by a door, or piece of equipment, or other potential source of sound. They would then bang on it, slam the door, or kick objects around the mill for a few seconds and then run back to the next person, where they would do the same. Each sound would echo through the mill and be enticing enough to pull Elmer and his crew in further. By the time the last person tripped their part of the trap, they would all be out in the woods, undiscovered, and Elmer would have all the creepiness he and his viewers desired. That was if it all worked.

"All set?" squawked the radio that Sheriff Taylor gave Jacob.

"Yep. Where are they?"

"They are doing their thing out on the road."

Jacob whirled his hand around in the air to get everyone's attention. That worked wonders. It made no noise, and at the moment no one was looking at him. He resorted to snapping, which did its job.

"Remember, give me two clicks on the radio when they head this way."

"Roger that," responded the sheriff.

Jacob stowed the radio on his belt. "Let's get going."

With that, they set off into the old, abandoned mill. It gave Jacob a bit of a chill just sitting there without all their little additions. It was creepy, and each breeze that traversed through the structure rattled some of the large doors and machines. The natural ambience was more than welcomed. Jacob had the radio, so he had to be first. He positioned himself at a door just inside the loading dock. From there, he could easily see Elmer and his crew's approach. It was his responsibility to set it all in motion. He had to make enough sound to pull them in, and then hightail it back around the corner and down the hallway leading to the offices where Sylvia was. His arrival would be her signal to begin. The sounds of the door and the distant footsteps should be enough to draw him in.

The longer he waited for the two clicks, the more he realized they really didn't have to do that much. This place was the epitome of creepy. Large, cavernous, and vacant. It was everything a horror movie would want. Plenty of things creaked and rattled all on their own. It was enough to make Jacob more than a little jumpy, and that said something. He knew Elmer was in for a real treat.

When they arrived, the two clicks on the radio echoed inside the old metal warehouse. Jacob took his position and peered around the door at the group of five that approached from the road. They were a long way away, but Jacob's view gave him a direct shot at them. There was no concern that the group would select a different entrance. The large open loading dock worked as a megaphone and projected the haunting sounds out in their direction.

Jacob watched as the man and his crew approached the mill. To him, it was like watching the show, but from the other side. Elmer wore a tan suit and a fedora. Trailing him were his two assistants carrying EMF meters and spirit boxes. Completely useless tools. A fact Jacob knew. He spent some time experimenting with them himself. They were splendid show though. The random blinking lights hinted that something might be there, and that was all Elmer's audience wanted. Now it was time for Jacob to hint at something that might be here. He slowly moved the door he stood by. It squeaked something horrible, sending shivers down his back. Instantly, all eyes, and the camera crew following Elmer's party, focused on his location.

Elmer Daughtry stopped and talked toward the camera. Obviously one of his monologues he did so often in the show. The other waited for him. Jacob gave the door another light push, producing a similar spine-tingling reaction. That got the group moving again. Jacob waited until they were just outside the door and gave a third and larger push until it slammed shut with an echoing thud. That would get their juices flowing and would probably send a few viewers reaching for a pillow.

With his job done, Jacob took off down the hallway toward Sylvia's position. The coolness of the old place and the sounds were still giving him chills, or so he thought. When he felt the first pricks just at the base of his neck, he knew there was something else. "Dammit," he whispered.

Halfway to her, he stomped a few times to give the sound of those distant footsteps you always heard on those shows. When he did, he looked around for the unwelcomed visitor that he knew was there. He needed to find it and deal with it before Elmer found his first genuine evidence of the existence of ghosts.

"They're coming," Jacob whispered as he slid to a stop next to his wife. She was inside an old office with a desk and a table. Both of which she held on to firmly to suppress their natural rattle until they needed it. When the time was right, she would give them a good push against the floor to produce a loud scrape. "We have a problem."

Sylvia looked back at her husband, puzzled.

"There's a real one here."

"Shit!" she muttered.

"Tell me about it."

Footsteps echoed down the hallway from the loading dock. They were inside. Sylvia pulled out her phone and triggered several Bluetooth speakers they had placed around. She would gather each on her way out to avoid discovery. Then she pushed the chair across the room; it gave a light scrape, but in this silence it was earsplitting. Jacob grimaced at the sound and covered his ears. For good measure, she did the same with the desk, and that was no less ear shattering. The light attached to the top of Elmer's primary camera shot down the hallway, and Jacob and Sylvia sat tight against the wall. When the light was gone, they crawled across the floor for the offices back door, and the back on the mill's production floor.

More pins stopped Jacob dead in his tracks. Whatever was there was close. The feeling grew and became painful. Beads of cold sweat developed on his brow. Whether they put on a good show for Elmer was no longer the biggest problem in Jacob's mind. He was now worried about Miller's Crossing putting on too good of a show for Elmer.

"I need to go find it," whispered Jacob. "Go on to Charlotte."

There was no debate. Sylvia continued on to the next post. Jacob only looked back once to make sure she had left. He was now squatting by a post, looking out for signs of their friend. In the distance, he heard Charlotte give the rusty six-foot diameter saw blade a spin. The sound of metal grinding on metal was ear shattering. There were three steps left for them. Through the glass walls of the offices, Jacob could easily see Elmer and his party move to investigate the sounds he and Sylvia had produced. From behind the post, he watched them place the spirit box on the desk in that office. They stood around it for a few moments before leaving, but not before they positioned a remote camera there, watching the spirit box. Jacob knew he needed to be careful to not appear on that camera. They didn't take the bait of the saw blade and again went into an office, a different office. He watched as they positioned chairs around the desk.

Elmer pulled something from his pocket and put it on the desk. Jacob recognized what this was. This was Elmer's EVP session. How long they would be there depends on how much they picked up. With the Bluetooth speakers producing noise off in the distance, and the sounds the others would make, he hoped it would be a lot. That would keep them isolated in that office for a bit, far away from whatever was roaming around. Jacob felt it was close, but couldn't tell an exact direction. The creep factor of this place was getting in the way.

Again, it was like he was watching the show from another vantage point. Seeing one of his crew pick up the recording device he pulled from his pocket earlier meant they were rewinding it to listen to something. Someone had heard some sound.

Then, in the office opposite of the one they were in, Jacob saw a flickering presence through the glass window. It roamed around, almost walking in circles. If any of Elmer's crew turned, they would find something that would change their lives forever.

Jacob whispered to himself, "Don't turn around." He said it repeatedly, hoping they wouldn't. He looked around for anything he could use to produce a sound, just in case, but the floor was remarkably clean. Behind him, deep in the mill, in the locker rooms used by the employees, there was a wailing. One of the Bluetooth speakers. Several footsteps went along with it, followed by a slam of a locker door. That got Elmer's attention, and he and his team scurried out of the office, meters in hand, and headed toward the locker room. Jacob watched as one person, one of the production crew, stayed back to position several other remote cameras for monitoring. He stood there in the office where they did the EVP session, and never had a clue that just a few feet behind him, on the other side of the glass wall, was an honest to goodness actual ghost staring at him.

Jacob felt a great sense of relief when the man didn't turn around, and the ghost didn't come through the wall. "Good ghost." Jacob remarked under his breath. Shortly after the man left the office, the ghost left through an exterior wall, and Jacob let a few more seconds pass before he headed out the main entrance. Going back to join the others was out of the question. The risk of running into Elmer or any of his party was too great. They were following the breadcrumbs that were being left. He looked back before he left and again saw them gathering in the darkness. Their lights gave them away. They were now doing a spirit box segment, and for no reason at all, that thing lit up and hummed like a rock concert. He left and thrust a single fist up in the air once he passed through the door.

Outside, Jacob sprinted into the woods, and then along the edge of the mill's property, hoping to rendezvous with the others. What he pictured as the others didn't include two full floating vapors and another walker. Panic drained him of any optimism he felt. The three were just inside the wood line around the mill, partially hidden them from view. He moved to see if he could divert them deeper into the woods, knowing he couldn't take care of them like he would prefer to. Doing that took time and could attract attention.

Jacob tried his normal approach by just walking in their path. The two floating vapors went through him. And then turned away from the mill. That was his suggestion based on how he stood. Something he realized long ago. Floating vapors hated contact with the living, and you could use your body to route them. All you had to do was stand there and angle your body in a way that when they pulled back from the contact with your body, they were heading in the direction you wanted. The walker was another problem. They weren't as easy to re-route and mostly had a mind of their own. This walker didn't move with the vapors and instead turned the opposite way and headed out away from the trees. Jacob ran to give chase. His hand reached for the cross in his jacket pocket, but he froze at the edge of the woods. It was too late. The walker was moving across the front entrance of the mill. Right in front of Elmer Daughtry.

12

"We have a problem. A big problem!"

"What's wrong, Jacob?" asked Sheriff Taylor over the radio.

Jacob was still hiding in the woods as he watched Elmer and the cameraman he screamed for following the flashing transparent visitor. He had an urge to run out there and intervene, but how? That was one question running through his mind. Another was more of a concern. Would he make things worse? Rushing out, cross and book in hand, would give Elmer a bonus he never expected. All he could do was hope the ghost would disappear quickly. Seeing him almost all the way to the road dashed that hope.

"We have a visitor," he replied. That visitor was floating across the road, eerily similar to the legend they created. The chills and pinpricks on his neck went away, but the figure did not. He was just far enough away Jacob didn't feel it.

"Can you turn them around?" asked Sheriff Taylor. "Tell them to let Elmer do his show and maybe they can get an autograph from him in the morning."

"Not that kind of visitor," responded Jacob. He emerged from the woods and slowly followed, keeping his distance. "It floated right across the road."

"Did Elmer see it?" Sheriff Taylor hastily asked

"He's following it."

"Shoot!" exclaimed the sheriff. Jacob heard the ding of the patrol car when the sheriff opened the door before the radio cut off. Ahead of him were several excited members of Elmer's crew. They were jumping up and down and doing everything but hooting and hollering. Jacob imagined Elmer might kill them if they did. He was enjoying his moment in the spotlight, and walked sideways in front of the camera, narrating the whole time.

"Come on. Go away," Jacob whispered to himself. Damage had already been done, but the sooner it disappeared, the better. They are now a place that will be the new spook capital of the United States, maybe even the world. Hundreds, if not thousands, of people will come to Miller's Crossing. They will visit the mill, and not the Scar. Jacob would have to take that partial victory.

Flashlights shined up the roadway as Elmer and his team crossed it. It was Sheriff Taylor and his father, still dressed as Deputy Miller. They weren't running, but they were walking with intent. They were attempting to intercept the crew of

Paranormal World. Why? Jacob didn't know, but he needed to find out, and picked up his pace.

Down the road, he heard sirens, and by the time the walker disappeared into the woods, two cars slid to a stop on the roadway. Now every deputy in the Miller's Crossing police department was on scene. Both Deputy Richards and Deputy Kline hurried to catch up with the sheriff.

Jacob reached the road and saw a rather animated discussion occurring ahead of him. He couldn't hear anything other than raised voices. The sheriff was remaining calm, while the production crew threw their hands up and around with every word doing most of the yelling. When he saw the first one go into handcuffs, that was it. Jacob took off running. He reached them after the third person went into handcuffs. There were two left.

"Stay silent everyone," announced Elmer. He held his head up, nose to the sky.

"Dad, what's going on?" Jacob yanked his father around by the arm. He responded with a puzzled look.

The crew exercised their right to remain silent as Sheriff Taylor and his deputies walked them back to their cruisers. Jacob again pulled his father back away from the group.

"Dad, what the hell?"

"Jacob, I haven't a clue. We were just sitting there when your call came in, and all he said was 'let's go' when he hopped out of the car. I just followed."

"Did he say what they were under arrest for?" asked Jacob. He turned to look at his father. Both men stopped and stood there. Over his father's shoulder, he saw their spook team standing on the other side of the road gawking at what was happening.

"He didn't say anything. He just told them they were under arrest and then put Elmer in handcuffs."

Jacob shook his head, confused. He had no answer. Not even one of the wildest corners of his imagination could fathom.

"We need to do something about that." Edward pointed behind Jacob.

When he turned around, Jacob found the source of all the issues had reemerged from woods. He had the cross and book, so it would be his turn. Not that they really took turns. He had taken over the family's duties from his father years ago. He walked closer toward it and finally saw it up close. It was the ghost of a teenage girl, and she didn't show any awareness that Jacob was there, which was common. At least until they saw the cross. They all noticed that. Some feared it. It drew some to it. None ignored it. This one was no different. It drew her closer. He took one look up at the girl and studied her face. He needed to remember it, so he could talk to others later or look Sharon Winters up in some old yearbooks at the school, just to be safe.

"Lord, accept this tortured soul into your good graces," Jacob said. He sensed no malice from her, so he didn't need to treat her as such. She was pleasant, but lonely. Those were the emotions that flooded him when she appeared. She dissipated quickly.

If only their other problem would go away as quickly.

Jacob hurried back to the road and joined his father at his pickup, that he had stashed further down the road to keep it out of sight. Edward was in the driver's seat, and Jacob didn't object, which was a first. Who could drive Jacob's farm truck was a kind of unwritten rule. It was Jacob, and only Jacob. There was far too much on his mind to object. All he could do was mutter, "This is messed up."

His father agreed and held out his hand for the keys. Jacob placed them there absent mindedly. His hand then dug into his pocket for his phone. When he pulled it out, he quickly dialed a number and held it up to his head as Edward cranked the truck and sped off, tailing the police cruisers. They passed Sylvia and Charlotte standing on the side of the road, looking as confused as they felt.

"Lewis, get the Father and meet us at the police station. Hurry." Jacob hung up the phone and then leaned against the door.

13

The drive back into town was a silent one. Which gave Jacob plenty of time to think about what had happened; or make that, try to. There was nothing, just a big empty void instead of the answer to why it happened, and the stark realization that what had happened just made things worse, infinitely worse. A point solidified by the scene that played out in the parking lot of the police department.

Sheriff Taylor and the two real Miller's Crossing deputies were leading the Paranormal World's production staff in through the prisoner intake door. Each of them cuffed, and appeared to be remaining silent, at least verbally. Their faces were anything but. They were stewing inside, and Jacob knew that feeling well. Only age and maturity had taught him to tamp down the eruption, and the realization that nothing good ever came from it. He seriously doubted any such eruptions from the crew would change the course of events.

The one member of the crew that didn't appear ready to explode was Elmer Daughtry himself. He strode in with his hands cuffed behind his back and his head held high. Jacob noticed his demeanor and thought it was odd, but it didn't take him long before he put two and two together and realized why. He had just videoed the actual existence of the supernatural, and now was being arrested for it. In the world of award-winning journalists, this was the probably considered a grand slam. Not that Jacob thought Elmer was an award-winning journalist. Even using the word journalist where he was concerned was stretching it.

Lewis's truck pulled in as the last of them walked through the door. Jacob and Edward walked over and didn't even let Lewis and Father Murray exit before they leaned on the door and the opened driver's side window. Both men looked at Edward, confused, and Jacob knew that expression was about to change to one of full out concern.

"Did we have problems? Someone show up?" Lewis asked, pointing toward the back door. They had pulled up just as the door closed.

"Well," Edward cleared his throat. "You can call it that. Taylor arrested Elmer and his crew."

There it is. The look of shock and concern Jacob waited for.

"Good God. Why?" Lewis reached down and opened the door. Edward backed away as it swung open with a loud creak. The passenger door was quiet when Father

Murray exited. Jacob had fixed that door a few years back. A retirement gift of sorts. The driver's side door had only picked up this habit.

Edward pointed at Jacob. He guessed it was his turn to deliver bad news.

"Several real ghosts showed up, and one of them crossed right in front of Elmer's team. They followed it across the road and into the woods. Recording it the whole way."

Father Murray's hand slapped against his forehead and remained there for a few moments before sliding up and through his receding white hair.

"That's when Taylor arrested them," interjected Edward.

Lewis walked over to the closest cruiser and opened the front door and then released the latch of the trunk. "And confiscated all their gear, I see." Cameras and microphone equipment filled every spare space of the trunk.

"Why?" asked Father Murray.

Edward shrugged in reply.

Father Murray looked at Jacob, and all he could do was shrug, too.

"Well, there is one way to find out." Lewis slammed the trunk shut and then marched up the walkway to the door. Jacob and Edward followed.

It was quiet up front in the lobby area, but the four men didn't stop there. They pushed through the half door at the counter and worked their way through the office. In the dispatch room, Sharon Randolph sat there with her back to her console, looking just as confused as the rest of them felt.

"Where is he?" asked Lewis. Sharon just pointed to the back, which was now beyond a door locked by a numeric code. It led to the holding cells, so security was a little stronger.

He reached down and punched in a four-digit code. The light on top of the lock remained red, and he grumbled as his hand reached and violently twisted the doorknob. It didn't give. That hand released the knob and formed a fist that pounded on the door. "Taylor, let's talk!"

It didn't take long before we heard the tumbler in the lock click and the door opened. Sheriff Taylor squeezed through the door, and then quickly closed it behind him. His hands sprung up in a defensive wait-a-moment motion.

"Now, I had to do something. You all saw what was going on." The man's eyes shot from person to person. "This was the only option."

"I didn't think this was an option at all," responded Edward. "Arresting them changes nothing. They still saw it."

"I have an idea about that," Sheriff Taylor responded. His eyes were still wide-eyed and continued to shift from everyone gathered around him. "Hear me out."

Lewis backed up against a deputy's desk and leaned back. He crossed both arms over his chest. "This better be good."

"We can seize and destroy their equipment. Say it is part of a criminal investigation, or they filmed on property they weren't given permission to use, which, technically, we only said they could film in the mill. The area across from it is city property. There was no approval to film there. It's trespassing."

Lewis let out a huff and stood up. The desk scraped against the floor. It made a second, louder scrape when he bumped into it as he walked around it. His hand gripped the edge, and Jacob noticed the knuckles on that hand turning white. "Mike, you can't do that. You can't do any of that. What were you thinking?"

Sheriff Taylor reached up and rubbed the back of his neck, but he didn't answer Lewis.

"Really? What were you thinking? If you had just let it happen, okay, that would have been bad, but we could have handled that, and even then, it did what we wanted. It steered all the rumors away from the Scar. I really couldn't give a flip who comes to explore the mill, but now," Lewis threw his hands up in the air, exacerbated. Jacob shared the feeling and turned around nervously, wanting to scream. "Now, all you have done is brought more attention to the town."

"Then maybe this all worked out." For the second time, Sheriff Taylor held his hands up, begging everyone to wait. "Hear this out. He found an actual ghost here, and we arrested him. Maybe we tell him we knew one was out there and hoped he didn't see it. The arrest was to help protect our secret. It adds to his story."

That sounded awfully flimsy to Jacob, but he wondered if he had dismissed it quickly because he knew what they were really hiding. He looked at Father Murray, who gave a quick shake of his head.

"We're the town who arrested him on camera," said Edward. "That in itself is going to draw more attention, and it is going to drive more conspiracy theories and stories about what are we really trying to hide."

"Mike," started Father Murray. "If we were really trying to hide the existence of a ghost out at the mill from him, why did we not only allow, not to mention help him in every way he needed? He will see right through it, as will others, adding more fuel to the Scar rumors."

Mike stood there defeated and deflated at the door. He was a man with no answers. The normal moxie that exuded from the sheriff was gone. He was now just a man that was having to face a mistake. The repercussions of which were yet to truly be known.

Deputy Klime cracked open the door, hitting Sheriff Taylor in the back with it. "Uh... Mike. They are asking about their phone call."

"Give us a moment, George," requested Lewis.

"All right." He closed the door.

"We can't hold them. You know that."

Sheriff Taylor didn't argue. His body language showed his acceptance of that statement, and he turned and placed a hand on the doorknob. "How about just for the night until we can figure out what to do?"

"No!" Lewis demanded. "Open that door and let's get them out of there."

Sheriff Taylor opened the door, but he let go and allowed it to close when Jacob yelled, "Wait!"

An idea had hit him out of nowhere. One that never even attempted to appear in any of his searches for an answer, but he wasn't one to hold a grudge. This answer arrived, and that is all that was important. "Fraud, or the attempt to create a fraud."

"I don't follow," Father Murray said.

"You arrested them because you saw what was going on and believed he was staging it, faking it. His broadcast of the footage and the fraudulent claim that goes along with it would cause others to follow, causing a disturbance to our community, and you didn't want our town to be any part of that. You can tell him you suggest he find another town to film his fake ghost in."

Edward slapped his son on the back. "That might work."

"It's the best idea I have heard," agreed Lewis. "Let's go talk to them. Give them a good warning and turn them loose."

14

"Sheriff, I'm going to ask nicely. We would like our phone call. I have an attorney in New York that needs to get on the road to come down here. I believe that is my right. The right to have an attorney present, correct?" Elmer said, sitting on the simple bench in the cell. He held his head high, but sat casually with his legs crossed. He had an almost relaxed and in control look to him. Not the image of someone handcuffed and locked in a cell. Jacob found it curious. He was on that side of the bars and looked like that, and everyone on this side seemed shaken.

There was silence while everyone looked at Sheriff Taylor. He stood there with the key in his hand, but didn't move except for the occasional quiver in his hand.

"Mike," prompted Lewis Tillingsly. His protégé didn't move. Lewis stepped forward, as he often did, to fill the vacuum of leadership in the community. Whether it was stepping back in the job years ago or small things like leading the fall festival committee, it was what he did, and what the community always looked for him to do. "Mr. Daughtry, I'm Lewis Tillingsly. The former sheriff here. You are absolutely right. You do have the right to have an attorney present during any questioning, and we will get you connected with him shortly. But I do hope you will hear us out first, and maybe we can avoid making this messy situation any worse."

Lewis held his hand out, and Mike handed him the key. Lewis stepped forward and unlocked all the cells, and then asked his former deputies to get Elmer's crew some coffee, and then asked Elmer to follow him so they could talk privately. The only room they could do so was one of the two interview rooms, and Elmer appeared apprehensive about entering.

"Shouldn't you read me my rights first? And I really want my attorney present for any questioning."

"Father, Jacob, why don't you guys go on in? Mike, you and Edward help the others." Jacob felt Lewis was trying to deescalate the situation by having them enter first. "Mr. Daughtry, this isn't a questioning. Just a conversation between men. If you don't want to say anything, you don't have to. Just listen, that is all I ask." Lewis flashed a wide smile. The same one that spent decades reducing family feuds to nothing more than a simmering disagreement.

Elmer took the offer and entered the room, although he was very reluctant at the sight of everyone on one side of the table and a single chair on the other. With a single look, Lewis instructed Father Murray to slide to the other side. Lewis slid the chair next to Jacob out and had a seat and then interlaced his fingers, placing both hands before him on the table.

"I want to apologize for Sheriff Taylor and how he treated you and your crew tonight, Mr. Daughtry. He acted a little hastily, but he had good intentions. As you have undoubtedly seen, we are a small town in every sense of the word. It's a quiet community. Now I can understand someone such as yourself has career aspirations, and there are probably many towns that wouldn't mind being part of those, but we don't want to be part of any staged hoax to help those move forward."

Elmer's calm and in control appearance disappeared. His eyes were wide open, and his jaw had dropped before he caught himself and clamped it shut again.

"The sheriff took you into custody to stop the commission of a fraud that would involve our town's name."

"Sir, there was no commission of any such fraud tonight. I assure you," spat Elmer. His voice had lost its regal reserve.

Lewis leaned back. A stern look spread across his face. "Mr. Daughtry. Don't take us small townsfolk as fools. Now you don't intend to sit there and try to convince us that what the sheriff and his deputies saw was real."

"It was. It was completely real. I assure you. We fabricate nothing on my show!" The regal reserve returned with a touch of defiance.

"So, if I were to take your show to some experts to analyze. They wouldn't find any added sounds, manipulated interviews, or any other adjustments to add entertainment value, would they?"

"Well, no. Nothing in any way that altered the facts."

"Let's face it. Your show is a form of entertainment. I imagine it's not uncommon to enhance things to draw the viewers in. Sports broadcasts have added crowd noise for years, and what was that one that fellow Geraldo did?"

"Al Capone's Vault," answered Father Murray.

"Yes, his vault. He knew it was empty. His entire production staff knew it was empty, but yet they sold it up big time about what could be inside. It drew millions of viewers."

"The insinuation you are making insults me. What we found and recorded out there was real. Completely real." Elmer Daughtry leaned against the table. "If you don't believe me, ask the sheriff and the deputy that were out there. They saw it with their own eyes. This was no camera trick, or green screen work." He leaned forward further and looked Lewis right in the eyes and stated, "It was real. Ask them what they saw."

"I have asked them. Sheriff Taylor said it looked like someone in a costume. They ran off into the woods before he could arrest them too," responded Lewis.

"What? The thing was glowing, almost see through."

"Maybe some of those LED lights underneath to make it glow," suggested Father Murray.

"So that is how it was done. Probably with some camera effects later to fine tune it."

"It floated just above the ground," blurted Elmer. He had the look of a man that was at his wit's end.

"They saw nothing of the sort."

"Well, it did," he demanded, losing a bit of his English accent. "It floated across the grass and road, and then off into the woods. And what about what I felt when it was around? My spine tingled, and I felt cold. It's a feeling I have felt before, many times, but only when I knew there was something paranormal around. Remember, I am a medium. I can feel things. I felt something as soon as I arrived in this town."

"Come now, you don't expect us to believe in that stuff. There have been stories after stories where science put it to the test and found nothing but hoaxes set up to rob people of their money."

"My dear Mr. Tillingsly," Elmer leaned back away from the table and regained a bit of his composure. "You mistake me for a parlor trick medium. The type that, for enough money, will get you in touch with your long-lost parents, or your beloved grandmother. That is not me. I don't speak to or for the dead. I feel them. Their presence."

"Now, I don't believe in such things," stated Lewis.

Father Murray looked across the table curiously at Jacob. Jacob felt he knew the meaning. Was Elmer really able to sense things? Hard to know, but being someone who does himself meant he couldn't completely dismiss it.

"Let's get down to brass tacks. We can't let you broadcast what you say you saw, which we believe you fabricated. The town of Miller's Crossing doesn't want to be part of any fraud, and the attention both positive and negative it could attract. If you destroy the footage, we will return your equipment to you. If not, then it will stay with us, and...," Lewis raised his voice for the first time, "if you think your big New York lawyer can take us to court and win, play it all out in your head. It will be a very public trial, with the footage released as evidence long before you can air it, and experts will examine it inside and out to determine if it is real or fraudulent. Now what would something like that do to your career?"

Lewis had given Elmer a lot to consider, as clear by the lack of any quick rebuttals. He sat there; a man lost in thought. His face contorted and strained with each thought. For a moment, Jacob felt for the man. He had made the discovery of a lifetime. Something that would make him a household name and was now being told he couldn't use it. If he refused, his entire world would be under a microscope, and Jacob had seen how this would play out many times. If you find one detail, one minor little thing that turns up to be false or fake, the media will run with it in a way that cast you and everything you touched as a complete fraud. There was no decision to make other than to agree. To not comply, put too much at risk.

"You are free to use the other footage you captured in the mill if you wish to salvage the trip," offered Lewis.

Elmer didn't answer, at least not verbally. They could all see the answer in his eyes. He knew it. He knew there was only one answer.

"And off course you will all have to sign a non-disclosure agreement that will restrict you and your crew from talking about anything that happened here, except what they found in the mill up to that point."

15

"And he agreed?" asked Sylvia, astonished.

"He didn't have much of a choice," yawned Jacob.

It was well past three in the morning, and the adrenaline of the night had worn off long before Elmer Daughtry finally instructed his team to delete the footage. They did it under the supervision of everyone else, just to be sure. Then, after they outlined terms of their release, Sheriff Taylor and his real deputies returned the crew to their cars and escorted them back to the Miller's Crossing Lodge. They assigned deputy Richards to watch over them, just to make sure they didn't take off under the cover of darkness. There was still the matter of the non-disclosure paperwork to sign with the town attorney in the morning.

Jacob headed home just before four, knowing he would get maybe two hours of sleep before he needed to be up to deal with his farm. The one downside to the long hours that sometimes came with his responsibilities. No matter how late he was out chasing ghosts, the farm didn't wait.

"With how Lewis put it, it was the only choice." Jacob pulled off his shirt and climbed into bed. "That man has a way with words. I certainly would have never thought about that angle."

"Me either, but he was right. Elmer's reputation is what drives the show. Any sort of investigation, with even the hint that he had faked any part of it, would damage his credibility. I seriously doubt his producers would continue to back his show if that happened. Not to mention the news headlines would have a field day with it." Sylvia agreed and then snuggled up next to her husband. "Get some sleep. I'm getting up with you to help around the farm in the morning. You must be exhausted."

This was an offer Jacob had refused in the past, but this time he was too tired, and let the silence relay his acceptance as he quickly drifted off to sleep, which was short-lived. His alarm woke them both two hours later, and they shared a collective groan. The farm never sleeps, echoed in Jacob's mind. It was a saying he used himself when Sylvia, or anyone else, commented on how committed he was to his chosen occupation. Now he regretted that saying. This morning he needed to change it to the farmer never sleeps. That was more accurate.

With Sylvia's help, he slogged through the morning chores, and it only took him an hour longer than normal. When he came back in, he collapsed on the sofa in the living room. Not something he usually did. His usual routine involved a quick shower, dealing with the business end of the farm, and then running errands. The evening was for sitting back and doing nothing. This morning, both his body and mind had rearranged his schedule without clearing it with him first. Not that he would have objected. He felt himself drifting off a few times, only to snap back when he heard Edwin in the kitchen with Sylvia. A stark reminder that his wife was working on less than a full night of sleep as well, and he needed to get up and help. Of course, he drifted off again before he moved.

The next time something startled him awake, it was with the help of Sylvia. She wasn't there to complain or ask him to help with Edwin. She was holding his cell phone out for him. Seeing the small silver flip-phone drove dread through him. When he didn't immediately grab it, Sylvia shook it in front of him and said, "Jacob, it's an emergency."

Hearing that woke him up enough to take the phone, put it up near his mouth, and mumble, "Hello."

"Jacob, we have a problem," said Father Murray. Jacob was about to ask him if the ghost was causing any issues, and if it wasn't could he just log where it was and he or his father would look later, but Father Murray's next statement forced Jacob to sit up. "Elmer's gone. His crew is still there, but he's gone. Sheriff Taylor checked the lodge's security camera, and saw him walking toward town just after seven, right past Deputy Richard's cruiser. He fell asleep at his post."

Jacob understood how that could happen. He was out there as late as Jacob was. "His crew is still there?" asked Jacob.

"Yes, so is his van."

"Are you sure someone didn't come pick him up?" Jacob asked what he believed to be an obvious question and swung his feet to the floor. His body protested his attempt to sit upright, and he leaned down against his legs.

"Not that we can tell. He was just walking."

Jacob looked at the old grandfather clock in the hall. If Elmer left around seven, he had a four-hour head start on them wherever he was going. If he met anyone down the road and got a ride, he could be in any of half a dozen mid-market cities sitting in front of a camera, ready to tell his tale. "All right, now what?" It had to be asked, but he knew the answer was not one he was going to like.

"Can you meet us at the lodge?"

"Sure Father. I'm on my way." He closed the phone and dropped it to the floor while collapsing back into the sofa.

"What is it?" Sylvia asked curiously.

"Elmer's gone."

"What?"

Jacob rolled his head forward off the back cushion and used the momentum to roll the rest of his exhausted body to his feet. "Elmer's gone. He took off walking toward town about seven this morning. No one has seen him since."

"And?"

That was the question, and there was only one answer. "I guess we go find him." Jacob stretched and headed to the stairs. He needed to get some of the pasture off of him before he went to help.

"Jacob, you can't. You're exhausted."

"So is everyone else," he replied with a sigh, and then headed upstairs.

Sylvia followed, with Edwin following his mother up the stairs, albeit slower. "Jacob, at some point, you have to stop and put yourself first. You were up all night, and then up at the crack of dawn working the farm. Most of them got a few more hours of sleep. Let them deal with it. Sheriff Taylor and Mr. Tillingsly can handle it. Rest."

Jacob knew he needed it. He felt wobbly the whole way up the stairs and needed to brace himself against the sink while he waited for the water to warm up. In his current state, he considered just washing off in cold water to shock himself awake. It would work, but for how long? Maybe it would be what it took to make him feel lucid again. All morning he had crazy thoughts and moments of wandering concentration. Both characteristics of the exhausted mind trying to keep things straight, but buried in all that madness somewhere between the fascination in watching one of his cows eat and wondering how many drops of water his sprayer was dropping every second on his crops as he drove pass, was a statement that Elmer made the night before. It was something that struck him when it was said, and even Father Murray took notice. After that he hadn't given it a second thought, that was until this morning when his mind wandering around the edges of rational thought, and again now it raised its ugly head.

Elmer Daughtry had said he felt there was something about this place. That he felt it as soon as he had arrived. Jacob couldn't dismiss that. He felt the same. The man also claimed to be a medium, which everyone who hosted the type of show he did made the same claim. Most of them had been proven not to be, or were so flamboyant where it was concerned, no one believed them, but he wasn't. He reminded you of his ability, almost like presenting a credential, but never, to Jacob's knowledge, had he fallen to the floor and shook claiming a spirit was entering him or anything like that. Could he really be someone who feels things? Could he be like his family? Why not? There was a town full of people like that.

It was a statement Jacob couldn't shake, and now, with the news that Elmer had walked off on his own, it brought a possibility. It was what Jacob knew he would have done if he were in Elmer's shoes, and felt what Elmer said he did, which he did.

If this was real, and not just Jacob's mind running away with random thoughts, the next possibility was horrifying.

"I'll be fine," Jacob said with a glance into the mirror. Washing his face didn't work. He needed something more. "Trust me. I'll be fine." He closed the bathroom door and started the shower, a cold shower.

16

"Any of his crew know where he went?" Jacob asked.

Father Murray, Sheriff Taylor, and Lewis Tillingsly stood together with Jacob in the parking lot of the Miller's Crossing Lodge, waiting for their guest of honor to return. Sheriff Taylor held an envelope in his hand, which contained the non-disclosure agreement the town attorney drew up very early this morning. All they had to do was sign that, and he would hand over the camera equipment he had stowed in his trunk.

"They didn't even know he was gone," said Sheriff Taylor. "They acted as surprised as I was when I knocked on his room to have him sign this," he held the envelope up, "and no one answered. By the way, his door was unlocked. That producer of his, she tried to call his cell phone, but he didn't take it with him. It's zipped up in his luggage."

"You don't think he had someone pick him up, do you? Walked down the road to meet them?"

The three men shrugged at Jacob's question. No one knew. Only Elmer knew, but he wasn't there to tell them.

Marjorie Tillman was pacing furiously up and down the walkway outside the ground floor of the lodge. Her cell phone pressed up against her ear, having what appeared to be a very intense conversation. Jacob watched her for a few moments while the others tossed ideas around. From how she was screaming into the phone, Jacob didn't doubt she was just as confused by Elmer's disappearance as they were.

"I have an idea," Jacob muttered. He thought he said it to just himself, but it was plenty loud, caused a few of them to call his name as he walked away from the group of men toward his truck. He arrived at the same time as his father pulled in, but Jacob didn't stop to greet him. He ducked into the truck and retrieved something he brought with him on a hunch. Part of him told him this was highly unlikely, but then again, was it?

He slammed the door and unfolded the map he and his father had constructed on their surveys. It was a normal road map of Miller's Crossing, but with points and labels based on events, encounters, and feelings his father and he had logged in his notebook, which he brought with him as well and placed it on the center of the map to hold the whole thing in place. By now, three curious men joined him at the truck. Edward was already identifying their current location on the map.

"Father, do you remember when he said he was a medium last night?" asked Jacob.

Father Murray nodded, "Well, yes. That is what he also claims to be on his show."

"And do you remember when he said he felt something off about this place? You gave me a little look."

"I did."

"What if he was right? What if he was like us? What if..." Jacob studied the map. "What if he did feel something odd, and he is searching for the truth?" His finger traced the route north of their location and circled several spots where there were regular occurrences of sights and encounters. "If I were him and felt what he does, and spent my entire life searching for proof of the paranormal, and finally found it last night, I wouldn't stop there. I would want to follow that feeling and see what else is there."

Sheriff Taylor pulled his radio off of his belt and keyed it up. "Sharon, it's Sheriff Taylor."

"I hear you, go ahead sheriff."

"I need you to help coordinate a search. I am going to read you a series of intersections that I need Richards and Kline to check out. Let me know when you are ready."

"I'm ready, but who are they looking for?" asked Sharon.

"Elmer Daughtry. I assume you know who that is."

"I do. I am ready for the addresses."

Sheriff Taylor stepped forward and leaned over the map. Edward drew a line across it with his finger. "Have them take the spots south of Route 37, and we can take the ones north." Sheriff Taylor nodded and then began rattling off intersections over the radio.

Jacob grabbed his father by the elbow and pulled him aside. "This could be a wild goose chase. It is just a hunch."

"What else do we have to work with, Jacob?"

A big fat nothing was what else they had to work with. He had disappeared into thin air.

"Sometimes we have to trust our gut."

"I know. I just can't dismiss the possibility that he is some kind of medium. It might sound silly..."

Edward waved his hands, cutting Jacob off. "Whoa, why would it sound silly? Jacob, this is an entire town of people sensitive to the paranormal world. There are six other places like this. They all feel something. It would be naïve to think there aren't others."

Jacob already knew that, but there was just something about accepting this that he had his doubts about. Maybe it was because the man publicly tried to pass himself off as a medium, as some sort of ghost hunter, and all the ones Jacob knew hid it from the world. It didn't help that so many like Elmer had been disproven and discredited publicly. They were just entertainers looking to con money from a believing public or to bask in the fame they could achieve.

"Jacob. Edward," Sheriff Taylor called. His radio was once again on his belt. Jacob and Edward rejoined the rest of them at the map. "I have them checking out every spot on here within ten miles. If we don't find him there, we will stretch it out. Father Murray is going to stay here in case Elmer returns. I am going to take this grouping here." His finger drew a circle around four spots to the northeast from where they were.

Edward leaned forward over the map, eyeing the same cluster Jacob was. Though there was another spot just outside of the radius of their search that had Jacob's eye. When his father claimed the cluster, and Lewis quickly claimed a group that was relatively close to their current location, Jacob eyed his other spot and saw three spots in that general area. They weren't the hottest of spots, one only ever having one sighting, but it was something, and it gave him an opportunity. "I've got these."

"Jacob, you don't need to worry about the Scar. Kline has already made a pass through there, and will again every half hour... just like normal."

"I know, sheriff. Those areas need to be checked. Not to mention it's the furthest away and I can ride through town and see if I feel anything else that, if this is what Elmer's doing"—which Jacob still had doubts about—, "might draw him."

"He is the most sensitive of anyone I know," stated Edward.

"Besides his sister," interjected Father Murray.

Even all these years later, the mere mention of her created an awkward silence. At least among those not related to her. Jacob missed his sister, and what Father Murray said was correct. Sarah was always more perceptive to the paranormal world. She could feel things miles away. Of course, she had a little extra help.

"All right. Let's get moving," instructed Sheriff Taylor. "Watch the roads for him when you're driving, and call either me or Sharon if you see him."

Jacob folded up the map and closed it between the pages of his notebook. He pulled off, not expecting any of them to find Elmer, but like his father told him. What other options did they have? He had other options; it was called sleep, but that wouldn't find Elmer Daughtry.

17

The drive through town wasn't helping Jacob's mental or physical state any. The town was about as sleepy as Jacob felt. He passed a grand total of two cars on the road, and less than five people out walking. None of them were Elmer Daughtry. There were friends that Jacob and his father knew well. He stopped to ask each of them if they had seen anyone walking by, and none of them had. Of course, that didn't mean he hadn't started this way and dipped down a side street somewhere. Jacob's plan was to drive out to the furthest spot, and then go a little further just to check the Scar himself, and then come back and work through the three spots in his area. On the way back, he would check out the side streets.

As he drove, he paid attention to his other sense as well. Nothing really pulled at him. There was that normal sensation he always felt, which got worse the closer he came to the Scar, but he didn't feel anything active at the moment. At least not in his area.

At Walter's creek, he stopped his truck and got out to look around. There it was. The place they worked so hard to protect. It was as desolate as ever. No signs of life. There were no weeds or grass. No animals at all. Birds avoided it, never flying across the creek. Best of all, there was no Elmer. It was peaceful, almost tranquil, with the creek babbling past under the bridge. Jacob would never let that sound fool him. This place was anything but peaceful. It was the home of the worst evil the world could know.

With nothing there, he turned his truck around and headed to the first spot. It was a pump house that helped provide the city with fresh water. The pump house itself wasn't the haunted location, but the area behind it was. It was a small brackish swamp that Jacob had been called out to three times before to deal with a visitor. He gave the city work crews that reported them a hard time. They didn't seem to appreciate it the first time Jacob did it, but that didn't stop him from doing it again.

This was the first place he went, not because it was the closest, even though it was. This was a spot he always believed may have been more active than the data showed. It wasn't like a residence where there was someone always there to see and report any visitors that made an appearance. Work crews only stopped by when there was a problem or some maintenance to perform. The fact that they had been lucky, or unlucky if you ask the crews, enough to cross paths every time had Jacob believing they were there a lot when no one was around to see them as well.

He pulled off Oak Street, down the rutted path back to the pump house. Squeaks and bangs from his suspension announced the large holes the recent rain had washed out along the path. Back at the shed, there was nothing, but that wasn't good enough to satisfy his search. He got out and walked around, and out toward the small swamp that was behind it. He saw and felt nothing. No Elmer, and no ghosts. Not even a tinge from something in the area.

Jacob's second stop, the Wallace farm, was the same thing. John Wallace even allowed Jacob to check out the locked barn. They only found one ghost out there once, not exactly a hot spot by any measurement, but Jacob felt he couldn't consider the search complete unless he checked everywhere.

When he told Jack what, or who, he was looking for, Jack chuckled. "He'd have to be pretty lost to find this place."

In a way, he was right. Jack's farm was stuck back in the woods about as far as any place could get. Only if you knew it was there, could you find it. Of course, if you had a feeling of something drawing you to it, you would eventually find the old path.

"Thanks, Jack," Jacob said as he trudged back to his truck. The lack of sleep was really wearing on both his body and mind.

"Anytime Jacob. I hope you guys find the fella."

Jacob hoped so too, but having not found anything so far, nor receiving any phone calls from the others, he was doubting there was any credibility in his idea. To start with, he didn't feel that was all that much.

His state of exhaustion was even affecting his ability to find the right gear in his truck. He had two more spots to check, and then he would call it a day. That was his plan, but how he felt at that moment made that plan feel like a stretch. He would do well to make to his next stop without crashing into a tree and becoming a ghost himself. Maybe Elmer would come study him then.

The third spot was the high school, which was a bit of a drive from the Wallace farm, but he was still the closest of everyone out searching for Elmer. It was also highly unlikely Elmer could have made it that far by foot, but that didn't mean he would actually be there yet. Jacob had to think about the route he would have walked from the lodge if there was something at the high school pulling Elmer in that direction, and hoped he would follow roads versus walking across open fields and taking a more direct path to follow his feelings. This was something Jacob gave a substantial amount of thought to while sitting at the stop sign on route 17. He felt rather silly about that, considering how little he thought about his idea, and that was decreasing by the moment.

Even more depressing was the realization that he needed to drive almost all the way back to the lodge to pick up the correct route he hoped Elmer would have followed to the high school. He sighed as he turned and headed back the way he came.

The lack of traffic on the roads this morning was both a blessing and a problem. Jacob didn't need to worry about hitting anyone if his attention waned, but that also meant he didn't have much to focus on, making it easier to lose his concentration. There were a few moments he caught himself swerving over the double yellow line, and then quickly jerked the wheel to correct his error. The farm truck veered again over the yellow line just before Jacob reached the edge of what they considered downtown. Instead of correcting it, he checked the lanes for any oncoming traffic, and when he didn't see any, he allowed it to drift a little more. He was following his internal GPS, and it was going off loudly now. Pins pressed into his spine before the chill arrived. That was a new sensation, but Jacob blamed his exhaustion.

At the next road, he took the right, following that feeling. This was not the next location on his list, but at the moment, that didn't really matter. If there was a ghost out there roaming around, he needed to take care of it before Elmer stumbled across it. He had already seen one, which they had accused him of faking, and negotiated an agreement to keep him from ever speaking of it. They might not be able to do the same if he saw a second, or if he saw others that they didn't know about, he could easily let their little secret out.

Willow Pine Road was not one Jacob had driven down many times. He didn't really know anyone that lived on it, not that many did. It was one of those roads that just connected two other roads that most used. He had journeyed this way once recently. He and his father had explored it as part of their survey, and there was nothing there then. Now was a different story. There was something, and the sensation was becoming stronger by the moment, or at least it was. The icy pins were disappearing one by one, and Jacob slammed on the brakes. He came to a stop with a squeal and sat and felt for a few seconds. If it was disappearing or moving away from him, he knew the feeling would continue to dissipate, but it didn't. It stayed the same. He leaned back against the seat and rubbed his forehead. This wasn't the time for a mystery. He already had one of those.

Jacob turned his truck around and slowly drove back down Willow Pine Road. The pins returned, and then they started going away again, but this time he noted where the change happened, and turned around and drove back to that spot and parked. He reluctantly opened his door and swung his legs around and out onto the road. There was nothing distinct about the spot. No road. No path. Just woods, lots and lots of trees and deep brush. This wouldn't be the first time he had to push through terrain like that to find out what was out there. He did it often. He just wasn't usually this tired, which made each step an exhibit of effort. Only the painful sensation of new icy pricks encouraged him to go on further. He was moving in the right direction. The thickness of the low brush was discouraging. Jacob was having to break or leap over large patches of vegetation with every step. What he wouldn't give for a clearing somewhere up ahead.

Jacob continued forward, and the pins continued to press into his body. The pain of their presence was quickly exceeding what he had conditioned himself to ignore. These were hurting. Just one more thing he wondered if his lack of sleep contributed to. It probably did, he surmised, and trudged forward, trying to ignore them and any concern he had.

Whatever it was, it was deep in the woods. And Jacob worried if it was moving away from him, leading him on a lengthy chase. With how intense it felt, he expected to have already run into it, but he hadn't, and he hadn't passed it. That he was sure about. Temptations to give up the search played in his head, but he knew he couldn't do that. When he spied a clearing ahead, he wished he had listened to those temptations.

18

"Holy Shit!" yelled Jacob. He didn't expect anyone to be around to hear him, but there was someone. He heard the movement on the other side of the shed that sat in the clearing he had just stepped in to. A shed that shouldn't be here. A shed that Jacob never wanted to see again. A shed that should be around five miles to his west, sitting among trees in the middle of the Scar. As strange and hard to fathom as it was, Jacob had no doubts that this was the same shed. It was. Right down to the peeling and faded paint, broken window, and scraggly bushes that were planted around it.

Jacob's hand plunged down into his pocket and fished out the cross he put in there before he got out of the truck. With a firm grip on it, he held it out in front of him at the end of his straight right arm. His hand shook, and this had nothing to do with exhaustion. That was gone. Thanks to the adrenaline the image in front of him brought, he was wide awake. There was a rattle beneath his feet. He actually expected that response to its presence. It had happened before.

Slowly he approached the shed, keeping his head on a swivel, not knowing what or who else might be out there. Working around to the front, Jacob found the familiar entrance to the shed wide open. His knees buckled at the sight inside. A single table sat in the middle, with two chairs on either side. A single candle sat in the middle of the table. He blinked and rubbed his eyes before he looked again. Hoping that when he did, there would be something, anything, different, but there wasn't.

He worked past the door, but never really took his eyes off of it. He couldn't. Fear wouldn't let him. When he reached the other side, he made another discovery that sent shockwaves through him. There, lying on the ground behind it, lay Elmer Daughtry, face down and surrounded by his various ghost hunting instruments.

Jacob froze at the sight and watched to see if he could see any signs of life. Slowly Elmer's back and shoulders moved as his chest expanded against the ground to take in a breath of air. Then they dropped as he exhaled. He was alive. Jacob reached for his phone and slapped on both pockets for it, but found nothing. He had left it back in the truck. There was no calling for help now. He was on his own, and he walked over to the stricken man, wishing he had paid more attention to the first-aid seminar at the local branch of the National Farmer's Union.

"Mr. Daughtry, are you okay?" He asked. His voice was nothing but just a breath. The building he kept glancing at had stolen away the tenor of his voice. There was no response. The man just laid there, but he was still breathing. Jacob moved closer and kneeled down, tapping him on the shoulder. Elmer rustled slightly.

"Mr. Daughtry, are you all right?" Jacob asked again. This time giving him a little shake on the shoulder.

"Not quite," Elmer mumbled against the ground.

Jacob stabilized the man's head the best he could, something he had seen on a sports broadcast before, and helped him roll over. He placed his head back on the ground. Elmer kept his eyes closed, but he moved his head around as if trying to see.

"What happened?" asked Jacob.

"Not sure. I followed a feeling all the way out here this morning, and I set up to investigate. Then you were here standing over me," Elmer said.

"You don't remember anything else. Like how you fell to the ground?"

"No deputy. I don't." Elmer attempted to sit up, but immediately slid back down to the ground. "I got to ask; how did you find me? This wasn't the easiest place to find, and I don't believe I left much of a trail, and I know you weren't following me. That deputy you had stake out the hotel was fast asleep when I left."

Jacob glanced at the shed again. He couldn't stop. It cast a menacing shadow over the two men. In a way, it cast one over the whole town. One thought drove Jacob–Get Elmer up and out of there, as far away from the shed as he could. It wasn't just for Elmer's benefit; it was for Jacob's too. Every moment he was there another sharp icy needle drove into his spine. The voice in his head telling him to run was becoming louder, and it didn't have a hard case to make. Jacob even considered leaving Elmer Daughtry there and taking off to save himself. It was a fleeting thought, but a thought, nonetheless. "We need to get out of here," Jacob said, still looking at the shed. He then reached down and grabbed Elmer under the shoulders and hoisted the man to his feet. He weighed a bit more than a sack of seed, and Jacob grunted as he lifted.

"That is it!" exclaimed Elmer. "You feel it too. I knew there was something special about this place. I felt it when I arrived."

Jacob ignored the assertion made by Elmer and threw one of his arms over his own neck. His other arm across his back and under his other shoulder. Jacob felt he had him secured and attempted to take a step. The man's legs didn't move. They hung there, and Jacob's step only dragged them that difference. If this was how it was going to be, there was no way he was going to get him through the dense woods. "Can you walk?"

"I suppose." Elmer took a weak step forward.

"That's good, now another," coached Jacob. He was taking one stride for every two of Elmer's, and even then, Jacob was lifting him and helping him with each step.

"It is this place. It scares you. Doesn't it deputy?"

Jacob ignored the question and lifted the man for another step.

"You are shaking. You feel that darkness that is here, don't you?"

There was a darkness all right. Jacob felt the massive paranormal energy in the place, and he knew firsthand of the darkness that existed in the presence that was there. His sister was the one that could identify the intention of the entity from miles away. Jacob didn't need her gift to know all he needed to know about this place. He knew it better than anyone. It had haunted him for years since his last visit. Nightly terrors, waking up and screaming. Many sending him hurdling to the corner of the bedroom where he would huddle down as small as he could and just sit and stare out into the darkness, hearing that voice. Each time, Sylvia followed him to the corner and sat and held him, sometimes rocking. All the while reminding him it was just a nightmare, that he was safe at home in their bed. Eventually he would hear her voice, and not its, and realize she was right. He was home in their bed, but that didn't mean he was safe.

"Let's keep moving, Mr. Daughtry." Jacob attempted to add gruffness to his voice, but it still came out sounding weak.

"You do feel it," Elmer Daughtry insisted. He then stopped moving all together, not taking the next step when Jacob attempted to lift him to assist. He stopped with his head turned in Jacob's direction. "There is something about this place isn't there, and you know it. Don't tell me you can't. I have spent a lifetime learning how to read people."

Jacob dipped down on his knees and this time used his legs and back to lift Elmer up and forward, forcing the man to take a step. He then repeated the act again, with the plan to continue doing that as many times as needed until they were out of the woods and back on the road, or at least past the door of the shed, which was what they were directly in front of now.

A cool breeze kicked up and pushed the two men directly toward the door of the shed. Around them, leaves swirled and then lifted high into the air. In the distance, a beast howled. Jacob recognized it right away and knew this wasn't a creature that lived in the woods. It was not of this world.

He forced Elmer to take another step. The man appeared to be nothing but dead weight. Jacob turned his head and fussed, "A little cooperation would be a huge help right now." Elmer didn't turn to acknowledge Jacob's request and appeared to be even heavier with the next step. Jacob struggled just to hold on to him, eventually losing his grip. Elmer dropped to the ground with a loud thud that shook the world around Jacob. He laid there like a heap of flesh that pulsated. Jacob stepped back and heard sounds of gurgling come from within the man. The skin on the man's exposed hands swole up to five times their normal size. When Elmer finally lifted his swollen and discolored head and looked at Jacob, his eyes bulged out of their socket. "I told you I'd be back, Jacob."

Inside the darkened shed, the candle flickered to life, and the swollen mass that was Elmer Daughtry ruptured and exploded into a heap of rotten and putrid smelling flesh that covered everything, including Jacob.

19

The explosion blew Jacob to the ground and sent him rolling backwards, head over heels. He finally landed against a tree on the edge of the clearing. His head cracked against its trunk, and he collapsed flat on the ground, looking up at the sky. Above him, the blue sky turned blood red. He forced through the pain to reach up with his hand to wipe the blood away from his eyes, but there was none. The sky had really changed.

Jacob rolled over and pushed up to his knees. The impact with the tree made him woozy. He was thankful he landed against a tree and leaned against it for support. He made another glance up at the sky, hoping to find a clear blue sky. When he didn't, he leaned his forehead against the tree, this time softer than its first meeting.

This had to be a bad dream, he thought, he hoped. He would even accept this being another illusion created by something evil. Maybe he was asleep in his truck and this whole thing with the shed and Elmer was a bad dream. That was it. He was so tired he fell asleep in his truck at a stop sign, or on the side of the road. Maybe he was still at the Scar. The question now, how could he make himself wake up?

Feeling his feet slide against the ground prompted a scream to wake up, but that didn't work. His feet slipped again, and he reached for the tree, but it was out of reach. His heels dug trenches in the grass covered ground as the force pulled him backward. Jacob turned around to face what he was being pulled toward, but he already knew where he was being taken. Even before his eyes saw it, he knew. It was the shed, and its open door sitting there like some monster waiting to gulp him into the darkness that was inside. Only the glow of the flame on a simple candle sitting on top of the table broke the darkness. Almost like a tantalizing lure.

Jacob dug his feet into the ground firmer, but he still slid right up to the steps. His feet hitting the ledge, and stopping, his body leaned forward and threatened to topple over onto the porch. On instinct, he held up the cross again, and there was a flash of searing heat. It threw him backwards again toward the edge of the clearing, this time missing the trees.

The shed burst into flames, and Jacob hoped that was a sign. Some kind of divine intervention against whatever evil this was again. Though he knew what evil that was. Elmer's last words clued him into that. He used a tree to again push up to his feet. A hand guarding his face from the heat of the blaze. Through the flames, he could still see the open door and the candle inside.

"Cleansing by fire," muttered Jacob. He remembered that from his history classes. It was why they burned witches back during the Salem witch trials. The only problem was the sensations weren't gone. In fact, they were growing stronger. Maybe this was the reaction of it to the fire. One final lash out, one last attempt in this world. He watched as flames consumed the entire building, eventually blocking his view of the darkness inside. A dark billow of smoke blocked out the red sky, turning day into night. Embers rode the column of air up. First a few, then bunches, and they appeared to swarm together. Eventually, Jacob realized they were not embers at all. They were screeching and screaming and moving around with purpose. The demonic creatures fanned out in all directions, and they kept coming. Glowing ember eyes with long black smoke bodies by the hundreds filling the sky.

There was a deep laugh from inside the shed, and Jacob took off running through the woods, tripping over bushes and roots the entire way. The creatures howled and screeched over his head. The sharp clap of thunder drowned them out momentarily. A red rain fell, and the screeching returned. Jacob reached the edge of the woods and leaped out of the tall brush, falling face down into a red puddle on the road. There was a familiar metallic smell when he wiped his face clear and stood up looking for his truck. It was several hundred feet down the road.

Jacob ran for it and slammed hard into the door, slipping on the ground when he tried to stop. He yanked open the door and jumped in and reached for his phone first before he tried to start it. A quick dial resulted in nothing. Another produced the same result. Jacob checked the screen and saw there was no signal, which he knew wasn't right. Every place, even the most remote places he and his father had explored, had a signal. A quick turn of the key brought his old farm truck to life with a roar, and he sped off.

Exhaustion was no longer a concern here. Jacob was wide awake, but he still crossed the center line several times as he looked out the window at the horrific scene above. With each swipe of the wiper, more revealed itself. A dark red sky, with a red rain that Jacob would swear was blood. Bolts of blinding yellow and orange lightning stretched across the sky with demonic, flaming fingertips that raped the horizon. Hordes of dark demons with glowing ember eyes zoomed across the sky, dipping down to the closest building. Jacob watched one break through a window into a house ahead. The family fled out the front door, leaving one hell and entering another. The creature followed them. Jacob pushed the accelerator as hard as he could, and the engine whined. Then he hammered the brakes, bringing the truck to a sliding stop before he jumped out in between the family and the creature. He held out the cross. Its glow blinded Jacob and sent the creature away.

"Get in your car and get as far away from town as you can!" yelled Jacob, but that family froze at the scene around them. "Now! Go!"

The father grabbed his wife and son by the hand and ran to their sports utility vehicle. Jacob followed them and kept their path clear. As they got in, he stood around it, his body swiveling around, holding the cross against whatever approached. Behind him, the vehicle cranked and backed out of the driveway to the road where other vehicles were doing the same, ignoring traffic laws and traveling at whatever speed they could to get out of here.

Jacob paid for his momentary distraction and was knocked to the ground by one of the flying creatures. He held up the cross as he stood and ran to his truck. With it outstretched, they would approach, but not attack. He made another attempt at his phone, first Sylvia and then his father. Both times the phone did nothing, and he glanced at it again and saw there still wasn't a signal. He raced against the flow of traffic back into town, now feeling torn. He desperately wanted to get to Sylvia to get her and Edwin to safety, but he also knew he needed to regroup with the others to handle this. A quick glance around made him realize how absurd that concept was. There would be no controlling this, and that answered his question.

An impact from behind rocked the truck. It sent Jacob skidding across the blood-soaked pavement, and he yanked on the wheel to regain control. He looked back, expecting to see a car that was fleeing and accidentally hit him, but there was no car. Just half a dozen of those black creatures, slamming into the back of his truck on either side, bouncing his rear-end from one side of the road to the other. One emerged up over the tailgate and moved into the bed. This view he had of it in the rearview mirror was the best look at one of the creatures Jacob had had. They appeared to be nothing more than smoke, with the vapors radiating out like octopus tentacles. Their eyes were glowing embers of what looked like coal. When they screamed, fire erupted from their mouth, scorching the back window. Jacob's pulse pounded in his ears, and he looked back at the road. He couldn't help but glance in his mirror from time to time as the war ensued against his back bumper. The truck's tires chattered against the pavement, struggling to maintain their grip. Each impact threatened to break them loose and send him spinning off into the woods on the side of the road. He quickly hung his cross on the rearview window, hoping the sight of it would provide him some protection. At first it seemed to work. It no longer felt like Mike Tyson was going twelve rounds with the back fenders of his truck. His reprieve was short-lived, and when they returned, they did so with a vengeance.

Black creatures swirled around his truck, crashing into it from all sides. Jacob could barely see the road, but he didn't dare stop. He couldn't. For his own safety and for the safety of his family. Screams of fire blasted against his windows and windshield. The glass kept the flames away, but not the heat. It roasted him from all sides, and he smelled burned rubber. He picked up the speed, hoping to outrun them, but they kept up with him, ramping up their assault. When the first one broke through the passenger side window, Jacob's heart jumped, and he jerked the wheel so hard he almost ran off the road. Then the others followed, smashing every piece of glass protecting Jacob, sending a deadly shower of shards over him. A hit on the front sent his tires skidding. Jacob yanked the wheel and pumped the brakes to bring it under control. Another round of fiery screams came his way. This time, without the glass to protect him, Jacob had to duck sideways behind the dash. He tried to hold the wheel straight, but when the flames hit his flesh, his arm jerked the wheel. The demonic creatures pummeled the fenders, finishing what his arm had started. The wheels left the pavement and the truck dove into the ditch, where it flipped. The dash and front seat were aflame, with the putrid smell of melting vinyl and burning foam everywhere. His body banged around between the floorboard and dash, battered and bruised, with the gear shift contributing several pointed blows before he landed on the ceiling.

Jacob attempted to sit up, but the flames from the seat licked at his face. He crawled in the direction of the passenger window, where water from the ditch was flowing in. Each movement provided a report of his injuries. Based on the excruciating pain, the injuries were everywhere. He pulled with his arms to exit through the window. A horde of creatures circled overhead, waiting. In a movement that made every muscle in his torso scream, he quickly leaned back through the window and reached for his cross. The heat from the burning seat above singed his arm, but Jacob ignored the pain until he had retrieved the cross and clenched it out in front of him. The creatures took notice of its glow and kept their distance. They had not when it was hanging on the mirror, which had Jacob thinking back to something Father Lucient had once told him. It wasn't just the cross that was powerful. It was the union of him and the cross. Perhaps he was too fast at dismissing that.

He pushed up off the ground and leaned back against the truck. Pain screamed at him from every joint, but best Jacob could tell, nothing was broken. That was except his truck. He backed away from it and got his first good look at it. It was upside down in a ditch. The attack, and the crash, crumbled into an unrecognizable heap of metal. Several of the devil's flock stayed on the other side of it, spying on Jacob. Their glowing ember eyes followed his every movement. When he moved in their direction, they retreated from the glow of the cross. This was a discovery he planned to use to his advantage. He just wasn't exactly sure how.

That was a question for later. He needed to get home. He needed to get to Sylvia and Edwin. That was the most important task in his mind. So much so, he even said out loud, "to hell with this town," dismissing the constant question of how he could fix this. Saving his family was all that mattered, and they were several miles away yet. Before he started off in that direction, Jacob made another quick check of his truck for his phone and found it, shattered screen and all, on what used to be the roof of the cab. This time he checked the signal before he dialed, and saw nothing, but that didn't stop him from trying to dial, and again the call didn't go through. He had no choice but to start walking in that direction, holding the cross out as the only beacon of hope in Hell.

20

Jacob passed house after house. Each abandoned. Each with the windows blown out, with tire tracks in the yard or driveway that were evidence of a hasty escape. These desolate and destroyed structures were once the homes of families he knew. What would happen now?

He shook the thought out of his head and focused on his own family, but that only lasted until he passed the first house burning. A demonic creature was perched up on a tree in the yard. It occasionally let out a scream in the structure's direction, adding to the fire. Jacob knew the home and left the road to check around the back. He hoped to find the back empty, no car parked there. It was, and he let out a sigh, Jason and Lily Stringer had gotten out, or weren't home. Because these were close friends to him, it felt a little more personal. Not that the earlier attack on him and his truck wasn't personal enough. Jacob felt the pull of home tugging on him. The worry and concern he had for Sylvia and Edwin, but that didn't stop him from approaching the tree and holding out the cross. He focused everything he had through his arm, and proclaimed, "Godless creature, you are not permitted in His world." The glow of the cross extended out along the ground and up the tree. Jacob thought for sure the demon would move before it reached him, but it watched curiously as the light crept closer. When it reached it, the demon disappeared. There was no great scream or scene of its demise. It just dissipated. Which Jacob found less than satisfying.

"Jacob!"

He turned back toward the road. There, in all the madness, was a long white Cadillac from days gone by. Jacob ran for the open passenger door and hopped in.

"Are you okay?" asked Father Murray.

Jacob just stared at him in reply.

"Um, yes," stammered the old man.

"Get me to the farm. I need to get to Sylvia and Edwin."

Father Murray paused before throwing the car into gear and driving on the road. There was no protest or suggestion of an alternative course of action, which Jacob expected. Father Murray would be thinking of the community needs, and not individual needs. The oath and promise Jacob made meant he should have too, but to hell with that. He needed to protect what was most important to him.

"The shed moved," Jacob muttered.

"What?" Father Murray asked, shocked.

Jacob quickly told Father Murray what he found out in the woods, about Elmer and what happened to him. All the while, the demonic mists of doom swirled around overhead with occasional exploratory incursions around the car, giving it a shove from one side of the road to another. The size and weight of his land yacht, which Jacob would have to guess was close to twice his truck, didn't deter them. The laws of physics didn't matter to them. They easily pushed the car anywhere they wanted to.

Car after car passed them going the opposite direction, out of town. Each showed wounds of being attacked. Father Murray saw a few crashed on the side of the road just east of the high school and pulled over to check. Each was empty. Jacob hoped someone else picked up the occupants and had taken them to safety. He didn't want to imagine the alternative. Father Murray ventured too far away from Jacob while checking and found himself the focus of several demons. They swooped down, knocking the old priest to the ground, where he hit his head on the edge of the pavement. A small pool of blood formed and mixed with the dirt and debris that lay right between where the pavement ends, and the shoulder begins. Jacob rushed over to him and helped him up. Father Murray sat up, but swayed back and forth.

"Let's get you out of here." Jacob picked him up and carried him back to his car. This time putting him in the passenger side. He was in no shape to drive. Jacob jumped into the driver's side and slammed the door. He propped Father Murray up and fastened the seat belt around him. Then he rustled through the glove box for a first aid kit or anything. All he found were a few handkerchiefs that may have been used, he couldn't tell.

Jacob pressed one to the gash on Father Murray's head. Blood soaked into the white fabric, turning it red. Father Murray swatted Jacob away, "Drive." His hand yanked both squares of white fabric from Jacob's hand and then tended to his own wound.

"Are you okay?" asked Jacob.

Father Murray responded to Jacob with the same blank stare Jacob had responded to the same question not that long ago.

Jacob pulled back on the road and floored the enormous car. His body leaned forward toward his farm, which was only a few miles away, to encourage it to speed up. The classic piece of Detroit metal had its own mind, though, and would accelerate when it wanted to. Its engine whined with an ear-shattering noise, drowning out the screams and howls around them. It didn't drown out the bangs and shutters the vehicle did when the creatures took aim at them again. Jacob had to work the wheel to keep the car under control. It wandered on the road enough when you were trying to drive straight as it was. Now creatures were crashing against it from all sides, sending it all over the place. Jacob would jerk the wheel one way, only for another impact to send him skidding the other causing another over correction, but against all odds, he kept it between the ditches all the way to the turnoff to his farm, and he yanked the wheel hard to the left. The tires screeched as they struggled to maintain contact with the road before they finally gave, and the passenger side rear fender kissed a tree on the right side of the driveway. Jacob could feel Father Murray stare a hole in the side of him. That would be another repair Jacob would make for him when this was all over. With all the work he had done on that car in the last decade, it was mostly his as it was.

It rattled up and over the rise in the driveway, giving Jacob the first view of his farmhouse. The sight chilled and enraged him. He slammed the car to a stop and leaped out, running the rest of the way. Two figures lay motionless in the front yard, and behind them, a fire raged in what remained of his home. He collapsed next to Sylvia's motionless body. She cradled Edwin in her arms. Jacob picked up both and held them on his lap. "Sylvia! Talk to me! Wake up!"

She didn't move. He bent down and listened. There were no breathing sounds for either of them.

"Sylvia! Wake up!" He shook her this time, and her limp arms fell to her side, letting go of Edwin. Jacob caught his son's body before it rolled to the ground and squeezed him against his chest. Trying as hard as he could to force life back into him, but it was no use. He looked back up the drive to beg Father Murray for help, but Father Murray was in no shape to help. He was hanging from a tree some thirty feet high by his collar. His body hung limp amidst a swirl of demonic, dark creatures.

Jacob turned his attentions again to the love of his life, a love he tried to ignore for this very reason, and bent down and blew air into her mouth. Her chest raised and then drop. He pushed on her chest, not exactly following the instructions he had learned in school. He pushed rapidly, not counting the compressions, and then bent down and blew hard twice more. Again, her chest raised, but then it fell. He positioned himself for compressions, but was knocked around from all sides. Jacob ignored them, and went back to the compressions, but again he was knocked away after just three. Two breaths again, and then more compressions, this time without interruption.

Tears flowed down his face, and he screamed up at the sky. He was angry. Angry at himself, angry at God, but mostly angry at the creatures that were now rushing at him. Jacob stood up over the bodies of his wife and child and held out the cross. They didn't stop this time. He muttered to himself, "Foul creatures, you are in our Lord's world. You are not permitted here. You are a sin against HIS good word and work," then he screamed, "I banish you! Banished to the bowels of Hell itself. May your soul rot for eternity!" Jacob's voice boomed, and a bright flash exploded from the cross and rumbled across the ground. One by one, each of the creatures disappeared, leaving Jacob alone on his farm. It was quiet when he collapsed back down to the ground. A single scream of a creature well off in the distance. Jacob didn't turn to look. He sat there, lost in grief, squeezing his hands into tight fists, before pounding the ground, wanting the world to submit to his will. To give him his life back.

It didn't happen, and Jacob collapsed down next to his wife and child, and begged for God to take his life too. He tossed the cross as far as he could, not wanting its protection anymore. Death did not come for him. Nothing did besides the sounds of others suffering. Jacob didn't care if everyone suffered. That wasn't his problem anymore.

21

"Jacob!"

Jacob heard his father calling his name, but he didn't answer. He didn't want to. Jacob had laid on the ground next to Sylvia and Edwin most of the day, but as night fell, he couldn't stand for them to be out in the chilly night air and carried their bodies into the barn. He placed each down with care on a bed he prepared with blankets, and then started up the heater to keep them comfortable. There he sat on a chair looking at them, his life. They appeared to be asleep, and Jacob wished that was it, but he knew. He had even accepted it. That didn't mean he liked it or knew how to move on with things. As far as he was concerned, his life ended the moment theirs were taken.

Again, he heard his father's voice, closer now. Jacob didn't respond. He sat there, watching over his wife and child. He wanted to be left alone, now, and forever. The sound of the lock on the barn's door turning drew a look of disgust before he turned his back to the door. It creaked open, and his father yelled his name one more time, "Jacob!"

Edward's footsteps echoed in the cavernous building as he ran to Jacob. He embraced his son from behind. "You're safe."

"They're not," Jacob said flatly, and ignored his father's attempt to turn him around for a proper embrace. He just dipped his head. His father's hands fell limply on his shoulders, and he sobbed. Jacob was beyond crying. This was deeper. Crying seemed like an insult to their memory. Not in the noble way, but it was just so insignificant of an act. Jacob couldn't think of one that was appropriate, though. There wasn't one, except sitting there beside them and never leaving them. Even that was way too little too late. He should have been with them to begin with. Their safety was his responsibility, and he failed them.

"Jacob, I'm so sorry," Edward whispered, barely above a breath.

"Not now, dad." Jacob stayed steadfast in his vigil over his family.

"What..."

"Dad, seriously, not now," he said. His hands were once again fists and pounding the crate he sat on. "All you need to know is I didn't protect them."

Edward's hands rubbed the base of his son's neck, and Jacob shook them off. Edward tried again, but Jacob shook them off again.

"Jacob," Edward started, but he never finished the statement, and Jacob didn't interrupt him. Silence did. There was nothing left to say. Nothing at all. Jacob knew that. He had nothing to say, and as empty as the silence was, it was comfortable.

Edward walked to the door, but stopped before he left. "Jacob, you can't blame yourself. This is not your fault."

Jacob now knew what to say, thanks to his father's remark and the anger he felt. He stood up, knocking the crate he stood on over with a bang. "Stow it dad!" His voice cut through the air and echoed among the wooden rafters. "This is completely my fault. I was supposed to be the one to protect them. That was my responsibility. So, you can stop your petty attempts at consoling me. It won't work."

Edward approached Jacob, extending an arm to embrace his son, but Jacob stormed away. "No, dad. You can stop it. This is my doing." He pointed down at Sylvia's and Edwin's lifeless bodies. "This is my doing!" he cried.

"Jacob. Stop it. They wouldn't want you doing this to yourself."

"Dad. How would you know what they wanted? I know they wouldn't want to be dead right now. I know that. And come to think about it. I should have seen this coming. Our family has always failed to protect their own. This goddamn stupid responsibility we have. You," he pointed abruptly at his father. His finger shook. Jacob knew he needed to control his anger, but he couldn't. Rage was brewing inside like a five-alarm fire. "You lost your parents just like this. I've heard the stories." He sniffed away tears, and his voice cracked as he started again. "And then you lost Sarah to a damn demon. Now this. Dad, this isn't a gift, it's a curse. We are a cursed family."

"Jacob," Edward begged.

"Save the bullshit, dad. I'm not buying it." He swung a fist at everything and nothing. "I'm not buying it anymore." Jacob took a step to stomp out. He wanted to leave to avoid any rebuttal his father was preparing to deliver. Whatever fatherly gem he had stored up for him, or an emotional message of console, he didn't want to hear it. There was nothing anyone could say that would change what he thought. If anyone tried to say anything to him, it would only push him further. None of their indoctrinated bullshit mattered. Only the facts of what happened mattered, and the outcomes of those facts wouldn't let him leave. He couldn't leave them alone. "Dad, I need you to leave," ordered Jacob. He pointed at the door.

"Jacob, you're hurting."

Jacob about lost his breath, trying to respond. Every muscle in his body seized tightly and wanted to explode outwardly. Edward was the only person around, and at the moment, Jacob gave no consideration to who he was. He stormed to just inches from Edward's face. His vision shook as he did so. Both hands clinched tightly, but held against his sides. "I'm hurting?" he asked rhetorically. "You think I am hurting? You're goddamn right I'm hurting! I'm destroyed, and you know what?

You're right as usual. It's not my fault. It's yours." Jacob reached up and shoved his father backwards. "It's all your fault. Yours and every one of our goddamn naïve ancestors that bought the story they were told hook, line and sinker. Generation after generation like a bunch of lemmings, marching right toward one family tragedy after another, and look now... it happened again. If you hadn't brought us back here, none of this would have happened."

Jacob grabbed his father by the shoulders. Edward appeared frightened and tried to pull away, but Jacob didn't let go. He held firm and forced Edward to face the direction of Sylvia's and Edwin's bodies. He wanted his father to get a good look, but Jacob couldn't bear anymore. He was ashamed for failing them, and bowed his head, hiding behind his father. "Get a good look. This is the latest family tragedy we blindly marched to. It was destined to happen, and we were both too stupid to not see it."

Jacob let go of his father and walked over to a corner of the barn the sunlight through the windows hadn't reached yet. "I want you to go. Don't say anything. Just go."

Edward didn't try to argue with him. He did as his son requested.

22

"I think this is what she would have wanted..." Charlotte said, and then caught herself and looked back at Jacob, panicked. Jacob didn't bat an eye, outwardly. Inside, he burned deep. He had heard many people say that over the last several hours as they decided on the funeral ceremony for Sylvia and Edwin Meyer. Since his outburst at his father two days ago, Jacob hadn't reminded anyone that this isn't what she would want, at least he hadn't reminded anyone out loud. "It's fine," he agreed, though he didn't know what he was agreeing to.

He felt a quick touch on his shoulder and jerked and looked up. He expected to see Sylvia as he so often had, but it wasn't her, and his heart fell another step down the ladder into the depths of despair.

"You don't have to do this," Alice said. "I know how hard this can be. We can handle it if you want to dismiss yourself."

Jacob had done well restraining himself as others made similar comments to him. He knew for a fact none of them knew how this really felt. Well, that was all except Alice. Alice had been married before she and Edward married. She lost her husband when she was in her late thirties. It was a car accident while he was traveling back from visiting family. She knew. She knew exactly how this felt. "I am fine, but thanks."

She rubbed his back. "If it ever gets too much, just let me know... and wait. I know it is already. Trust me, I know. I mean, if being here is too much, just let me know and I will handle everything. Sylvia is a wonderful woman. A wonderful wife and mother, and Edwin is such a joyous child. I will make sure their memory is honored."

Jacob appreciated the fact that she said 'is' instead of 'was' when talking about them. He knew why she did it. "Thank you, but I need to be here. I need to do this for them."

He felt the warmth of a hug from his stepmother, but noticed she stayed close. There was something else on her mind, and he was standing in the corner. "And Jacob, can you give your dad a break?"

"Not now Alice, please." Jacob wasn't in the mood.

"I am only going to say one thing more. He told me what all you said."

"Let me stop you there," Jacob interrupted her. He had had some time to think about what he had said to his father. Time hadn't changed the emotions he felt, and still did, or most of what he meant, but there was one slight correction he had to make. "I know this wasn't his fault."

Alice gave Jacob a little pat on the back. "Talk to him. You guys have always been so close."

There are well meaning concessions, and there are those just to make someone stop trying. "Okay," was the latter. Jacob knew he would talk to his father. The question was when, and he didn't have a timetable for that, and wasn't ready for anyone else to impose one. He meant everything he said besides what he had already acknowledged. They were cursed, and he was right all along.

He was right for ignoring Sylvia for all those years. He was right for thinking he needed to stay alone. If he had stuck to his guns and ignored all the others telling him he deserved to find "happiness" she would still be alive. There, again, was a reason her death wasn't his father's fault. It was his, without question.

"Alice, can I bother Jacob for a moment?" Father Isaac asked.

Alice got up, but not without placing a rather motherly kiss on Jacob's forehead. He appreciated the gesture and attempted to return a smile, but was sure it was nothing more than a more relaxed frown.

"Father, we have already talked about the service. It just needs to be traditional."

"Jacob, it's not about that. Can you join me in my office?"

Jacob didn't want to, but it removed him from the room of a thousand woeful glances. Whether it was from his family and friends that helped him make arrangements for Sylvia and Edwin, or the over three dozen other families that were passing through doing the same thing. Each of them grieving. Each of them looking at Jacob as they did, knowing he lost his family, but also knowing it was his responsibility to save theirs. Jacob didn't know for sure they were all thinking that, but that didn't matter. His mind was convinced they each were.

"What is it, Father?" Jacob asked, as he entered the small office with a desk and two chairs. Father Murray had never used this room for such. It was just storage when he was in charge. If you needed counsel or to talk to Father Murray about any church business, it happened around his kitchen table or in his living room. He was warm like that. He was as warm as a summer evening. Perfect to sit around and share stories with, but always teaching. Father Isaac was, well, there wasn't another word Jacob could think of to define in other than clinical, and that was how his office appeared too. There was a simple wood topped desk, two folding chairs on one side of it, a desk lamp, the type that had an arm that extended so you could position the light where you needed it, and a gray metal filing cabinet in the corner. He kept it tidy, leaving nothing out on the desk, which is why this time was so odd. There was something on the desk. There were two something on it, and Jacob sat as far away from them as possible when he picked which of the two chairs he sat in. That book and that cross had caused enough damage. It didn't help.

"Jacob, I believe these are yours." Father Isaac leaned forward and slid the old brown leather-bound book and beat-up cross toward Jacob. "Your father found them."

Jacob sat there, staring at the two objects. The two objects that at one time defined him, but now were what had destroyed him. He didn't lean forward for them. Instead, his posture straightened, putting more space between himself and them, but even at this distance, his hands could feel the objects. The rounded corners and worn grain of the old cross. The weight of the book. He had spent so much time reading and updating the book, he could identify every page by how it felt to his fingers. The feeling was familiar, a connection to his past. That was what it was. Now just the memory of how it felt threatened to bring the bile in his stomach rolling up.

"Jacob, your father also told me about your conversation." He grimaced as he put air quotes around the word conversation. "I can completely understand how you feel. Jacob I really can."

Jacob looked away from the fake expression of sympathy. This was where Father Murray was light years better than Father Isaac. When Father Murray said he cared, or he understood, he really did. There was nothing not genuine about him, and now the man was gone. Jacob chalked it up as another failure of his. The loss was not only personal to him, but personal to everyone in the community. Father Murray was a pillar of the town. The rock that held it all together. A close family friend of all, and enemy and stranger to none. Now, with this town dealing with so many deaths, was a time when they needed him most, but he was gone, all because Jacob failed. At least, that was how Jacob saw it. Who they had left was nothing more than an internet church hack. Yes, the Vatican sent him over here with the highest praise. They urged Jacob to get to know him, to view him as a mentor. The first time Father Isaac saw a genuine ghost, he turned and ran. That ruined any chance he would ever be Jacob's mentor right then and there. From that point on, Father Isaac stayed out of that side of Miller's Crossing, leaving it to his predecessor.

"Jacob, I hate to ask this, but we need you back out there. Those things come back every night, and I don't have to tell you people are more than a little frightened."

Jacob fought the urge to roll his eyes at yet another example of how Father Isaac didn't get it. Jacob knew the constant sarcastic dialogue playing in his head was just one of the phases of grief, or he hoped. Father Isaac had already given him the textbook explanation of all the phases and what Jacob would feel over the next several days to weeks. He delivered it with all the warmth and compassion of the paper he read it off of.

"We all know you are hurting, and I know that hurt has turned into hatred toward what caused all this. You may even feel some self-doubt, and that is to be expected."

Anticipation of the pending request made Jacob cringe.

"We need you and your father back out there..."

"I'll pass," interrupted Jacob. He didn't even look at the priest.

"Jacob, I don't think you understand." Father Isaac stood up and walked around the desk. He leaned against it next to the book and the cross. His hand reached down and inched them closer to Jacob. How he bent down to look Jacob in the eyes annoyed him. Jacob wanted to blurt out that he understood all too well, but the collar that man wore demanded some semblance of respect, or at least restraint.

"Father, I do understand." Jacob didn't elaborate, leaving an awkward silence between the two men. Father Isaac fidgeted with his hands, while Jacob sat there stone still. Jacob was wondering who would flinch first. Any flinching by Jacob would be him walking out of the room. This conversation was over as far as he was concerned.

The loser, first to flinch, was Father Isaac. He reached down and grabbed the book and cross and held them out to Jacob. "Good. Then you are going to need these back. It is your family's duty."

For the first time since Jacob entered the office, he made eye contact with the priest. It was a cold icy stare that set Father Isaac back. Jacob stood, and Father Isaac's eyes followed and looked up at him. His hand still held the book and cross for Jacob to take it.

"Father, you misunderstood me. I do understand. I understand far too well. Look at what this has cost me. Look at what it has cost my family. My wife. My child. My sister. My grandparents. I am sure there are others in my family that lost their lives because of this that I don't know about. This isn't a responsibility. It's a curse, and I'm done with. You can give me that righteous bullshit speech all day long about duty, and responsibility, or some crap about the higher purpose. What you will never understand is the sacrifice, the costs, but..." Jacob reached out and ripped the book and cross out of Father Isaac's grip. He regarded them for a second, and then shoved them back to Father Isaac's chest. "You should understand. The Vatican chose you to come and counsel us. You know everything about all this, and if you think this is so important, then you take care of it."

Jacob didn't wait for the priest to grab the books, and let them fall down at their feet, and then walked out of the office. He stopped where Charlotte and Mary Summer were discussing the details of the funeral. "Everything set?"

"Yes," Charlotte said.

Jacob bent down and hugged her. "Thank you." When he did, he could see Father Isaac standing in the doorway, shocked. The book and cross were in his hands.

23

Jacob returned to his farm. During the drive, he checked the rearview mirror often for his father's car or anyone else that might follow him to attempt to talk some sense into him. It would be fruitless, in Jacob's opinion. He felt there was a lot of sense in his decision, and there really wasn't anything anyone could say to convince him otherwise.

When he pulled off the road and up and over the rise in his driveway, he brought Father Murray's Cadillac to a stop. In front of him were the ruins of his life. There was the spot where he found his wife and child lying lifeless. It was a spot that held enough significance that he avoided walking anywhere near it each time he passed. Beyond it, the charred remains of his family's home. His great grandfather built that house, or so he was told. Tears ran down his face. It was the first time in two days. He thought there were no more tears left to cry, but as they flooded his vision, it appeared there were more than enough left. He leaned his head down against the steering wheel and wept.

Home was no longer home. It was just a place. A place of painful memories and nightmares. Jacob hated pity. That was why he turned down Alice's offer to let him stay with them for a bit. Others made a similar offer, and he turned those down as well. This was where he belongs, or down the two fresh ruts he carved out through the field that led back to his barn was where he belonged. The small room he fixed up with a mattress and a refrigerator was home now. What was the saying? Home was where you laid your head. To him, it had been so much more than that, but now that was all it was, and probably all it ever will be again.

He parked outside the barn and walked through the door, never looking to his left where he had laid Sylvia and Edwin. That place was as off limits to his psyche as the place where he found them. It wasn't an attempt to forget about them. It was all about pain management, and he was already on overload. Any more could cause a break. He changed quickly and went to the only thing he had left, his work on the farm, which he had neglected over the last two days.

It took him about twice as long as normal to get things under control, but unlike before, he could never lose himself in his work. Thoughts such as wanting to let Sylvia know he would be out there longer than normal crept into his mind. She knew his schedule and if he was late by even as little as thirty minutes, she would come out to check on things. She knew Jacob was a schedule keeper, and if he was late, something would be wrong. His eyes even glanced up the hill a few times where she would stand just outside their home. He never saw her and was thankful he didn't see something else either.

His father told him about how he saw their mother only a few times after she died. Jacob didn't fully understand how painful that would be until now. Just the thought of seeing her that way sent shivers down his body and tears flowing from his eyes. Would he see Edwin? That was another one he knew he would never be ready for. Even seeing someone like Father Murray would be painful. Every spirit he saw before was a stranger. This had become personal.

Thoughts of what next circled the drain of his consciousness. They were fleeting thoughts. Ones he needed to make decisions around, but ones he wasn't ready to make. He couldn't see beyond the farm. He really couldn't see beyond the next few moments.

As the sun went down, he rode his tractor into the barn. Just like the past two nights, the clouds returned, and the sky turned red. This wasn't mother nature painting a portrait. There was nothing natural about this. He sat and watched until he saw the first signs of their visitors flying around. Their ember eyes glowed against the dark red sky. Screams of fire shot down from the sky, but Jacob didn't hear the horrifying wail or screams. They were miles away, and just like the last two nights, they wouldn't come any closer to his farm. They were only there the first day, and then vanished when Jacob lost it. Every night since, he has seen a clear night sky overhead, and the moon had even passed by before disappearing behind the clouds that sat over the town.

There was a rattling in the barn as he put away the tractor. His cellphone vibrated constantly on the bench where he left it. The cracked screen glowed showing incoming call after incoming call. A few text messages broke up the stream of alerts. He didn't check them. He hadn't touched the phone other than to plug it in since that night. There was no one left to call him he would care to hear from.

He spent his night watching the old console television that was in the house when his father brought them back here so many years ago. Both Sarah and Jacob objected to having to deal with an antique like that, and Edward didn't put up much of an objection, replacing it and storing it in the barn as soon as he could. The channel selection was limited to what he could pick up on the digital antenna he installed on top of the barn years ago. Sylvia called this his man-cave, though he didn't use it that way. The television was only on there to provide some ambient sound while he worked on something out there. Lucky for him, the barn was on a high spot on the property, which gave him a few more channels from neighboring towns. He clicked through the channels over and over, using the dial on the front of the console. Nothing caught his interest. Nothing would. Not even a playoff baseball game, which wild horses wouldn't have been able to drag him from before.

The background noise of the television helped Jacob zone out and find a few, albeit brief moments, of an empty mind. Memories of Sylvia's voice calling him brought him back to his painful reality. He didn't want to hear it, but at the same time, he never wanted it to stop playing in his head. He was the same way with his mother. The fear of forgetting her was always present, and it took a while for the pain of the loss to go away, allowing him to cherish those memories. A banging on the door replaced her voice, and Jacob let his head collapse down to his hands. For a moment, he ignored it, hoping it would go away, but it didn't. The second banging told him it wasn't going away until he answered it.

Jacob trudged to the door and opened it. His father stood on the other side with Deputy Richards, make that Sheriff Richards. The former deputy now wore the sheriff's star and a hat similar to what Lewis Tillingsly had when he served. No one had to tell Jacob what that meant.

Jacob didn't extend any formal invite, and just walked back to his makeshift bed leaving the door open. The two men followed.

"Jacob, things are real bad out there," his father started.

"They're not that much better in here," Jacob muttered under his breath.

"We need your help," finished Edward, unaffected by his son's comment.

"Jake, we really need your help. We've evacuated everyone to the gym for the night, and your father and Father Isaac put down some holy water that seems to keep them away, but we don't know how long that will work."

"And eventually they will stop coming only at night, and come during the day," added Jacob. "Tell me. How is Father Isaac doing? Tell me, has he come face to face with them yet?"

"Jacob, knock it off," admonished Edward. "He is a little green, but we all start that way."

"Isn't he supposed to be an expert?" Jacob had seen that look on his father's face only a few times before. He knew he was pushing things and leaned back against the wall his bed was next too.

"Jake, are there really any experts? It just takes time. You know I pissed my pants the first time I saw one," said now Sheriff Tony Richards, a classmate and high school baseball teammate of Jacobs.

"But Tony, you were thirteen, not some expert trained by the Vatican for this."

Edward found the one chair in the barn and slid it up close to his son and sat. "Look, we can play this game all day long, and it isn't going to get us anywhere. No, Father Isaac isn't ready for this. There is no arguing about that, and he has already called the Vatican for help."

Jacob sighed loudly at hearing the young priest had thrown in the towel.

"But," Edward said loudly, "We are ready for this. We are the experts, but I need your help." Edward reached into his jacket pocket and pulled out a familiar folded up paper. "I have checked a few of these spots during the day, but I'm not finding anything." He unfolded the map he and Jacob had created together. The last time Jacob saw it was in his truck, which, to his knowledge, was still lying upside down in a ditch.

"It's not on the map," Jacob said without even looking at it.

"Then show me." Edward threw a black Sharpie down on the map.

Jacob glanced at the location on the map. It was empty. He could put the dot there, but he knew what would happen next. First, his father would ask him to come with him, which Jacob would refuse. There would be a lot of conversation about it. Possibly even some screaming and yelling before his father would leave. Then Edward would go out there on his own, which Jacob felt would be a march to his death, and he didn't want to be any part of that. Book and cross be damned. They were powerful, but Jacob saw firsthand what happened to him, even when he had both.

"I don't know where," lied Jacob.

His father stepped forward and pressed his finger down hard on the map, causing it to crinkle. "I know it is in this general area." Edward's finger circled the spot on the map. "We saw the column of smoke. It was in the area you were investigating..."

"I know. I saw it too," Jacob said, interrupting his father. "I was over here and heading to this spot here by the high school." Jacob pointed to two of the three spots he volunteered to check out. He looked at the roads that crisscrossed the map for a plausible detail in his story. "I was here just north of Ingleside Court when I saw the same column of smoke." Where Jacob picked, put him well outside the circle his father had just drawn with his finger. "I tried to get back home when I was attacked by those things. Since you found the map, I'm sure you saw what happened to my truck." Jacob looked at both of his visitors for acceptance of his story.

"Then help us find it, Jacob," requested Edward.

"Dad, I can't."

"Jacob, we need you."

Jacob stood up from his mattress and walked to the workbench across the room. His hands rested on the surface and fiddled with a few of the objects that sat on it. This was the fight he knew he couldn't avoid, no matter if he told him where it was or not. "Dad, I can't. I'm done with this. I've already told you this."

"Son, I know you are hurting. We all are, but this is bigger than us. If you want to quit, then quit after this, but right now, we need your help." Edward walked over and placed both the book and cross on the bench next to Jacob.

Jacob ignored them, or tried to. He knew they were there, but made sure not to look at them. "Dad, I can't." At that moment, Jacob bowed his head. He had never refused his father before and he knew this time he was refusing more than him. He was refusing the entire town.

"Jacob, you don't really have a choice."

Jacob spun around, surprising his father and Sheriff Tony Richards. He pointed a finger, which shook. That last statement stung and stung deep. There was an avalanche coming, and Jacob lacked the strength to hold it back. "Actually, I do. We always did, and we always made the wrong one. Your father had a choice, but made one that cost you their lives. You had one, and that cost Sarah her life. I had one, and to be honest, I almost made the right choice, but gave in, and now look what happened. Dad, we all had choices. We just all made the wrong one, but I am fixing that now. I am fixing that right now."

Edward stormed over to the door and kicked it open. Through the opening, the red sky was clearly visible. "Jacob, we have a responsibility to fix this. This is bigger than you, me, or our family right now. The lives of hundreds of families are at stake, and we are the only ones that can help them."

"Help them, how dad? We aren't experts. You know that better than I do. Remember, you told me the story about when Father Murray admitted that all this was just guesswork. So don't try to act like you have bought in to all of this. Even if we could find the source, what are we going to do? Throw ideas and prayers at it until something works? It's a suicide mission."

"We have to try," his father yelled back.

"No dad. We don't. There are experts in this stuff out there. Father Isaac can call one of them in. You were never trained. I was, and nothing Father Lucient taught me covers how to handle this." Jacob walked out the door. He pointed up at the sky in the distance. "This isn't what we were sent here to handle. We were here to keep the peace between the worlds of the dead and the living. That was what Father Lucient explained was our assignment. This is not that. This is way beyond that. When I look out there at what is happening, I see the verses of Revelations playing out right in front of me." Jacob walked back inside and let the door close behind him. "Dad, face it. The world is a shit show. Everyone hates everyone. There is no respect for the individual anymore. There are examples of it in everything you see. Maybe this is the end."

This was something Jacob had thought about while riding the tractor on the farm today. His mind playing through every verse of the book of Revelations, and he realized how everything described was happening. Whether it was something that was happening elsewhere in the world, or what was happening right here in Miller's Crossing, it all lined up. If you walk around a big city, you don't have to go far before you find someone with a sign that says—The End is Near. Most consider that person a crazy coot, but perhaps they were the ones that were right all along.

"Jacob, you can't believe that."

"Dad, look all around you."

"Where is my son that hoped for the best in people? My son that was always willing to help others."

Jacob turned his back to his father. "Maybe his hope died, and he finally sees the truth."

"Jacob," started Sheriff Richards, but Jacob heard his father stop him. He knew what his father was thinking. He was thinking his son just needed time. That this was a grieving man speaking, and he was right. Jacob was grieving. He was grieving deeply, and yes, there was no hope left in his heart. Jacob was aware this could be a temporary condition, but that didn't change the fact that his eyes were opened, and he finally saw the truth. It was something that demon that he believed was the devil himself said while he sat on the other side of the table from him in the shed. Was it right? We were created in HIS image, and we were flawed. Was God flawed? Was life flawed? Were all these beliefs just illusions to keep you from seeing the flaws of humanity? Was all this just an illusion?

"Jacob, son, look at me."

Jacob turned around slowly. He expected to see his father's scowl. It wasn't a look Jacob saw often, but he didn't. He saw a broken man, and that tore at Jacob more than the scowl would have. "I understand. I do. We have a job to do here, and I am going to go out and try. Will you think about coming to help?"

Jacob started to answer. He was going to give an emphatic no.

"Doesn't have to be tonight. Maybe tomorrow. All right?"

Jacob agreed without a thought, which he later regretted. He should have said no. It was a hard no, but there was something about the way his father asked him that produced that reaction.

24

This was the moment Jacob had dreaded the most. He sat in the front seat of Father Murray's Cadillac. Just one of many cars parked along the road in Miller's Crossing Memory Gardens. This was the second day of what was a continual funeral for the town. Some came and went, others stayed through all of them to honor and remember those that had died. Jacob had skipped the first day. That was the day he was making the preparations for this day, but there was one thing Jacob failed to prepare himself for. The looks he would get when he arrived.

He fully expected to see the looks of pity and sympathy. It would be odd if he didn't. But those weren't the looks he saw. At first, he thought the looks coming from the people parading past were because of what he was in. This was Father Murray's car. This long white Cadillac with all the dents and dings in it was a fixture of the community. It was the vehicle that brought compassion and support. The chariot of faith that over fifty years had helped everyone in the town. Jacob wasn't blind to that, and while there were many holes in his heart for his loss, the one for Father Murray was no less significant than those of Sylvia or Edwin. He was family, as was Lewis Tillingsly, who was laid to rest the day before. Jacob couldn't force himself to attend it. If that were *that* look, Jacob could have accepted it, but it wasn't.

Jacob waited for the mass of people to pass by before he exited the car and followed them at a distance. He even stood away from the gathered masses, over by a tree, for the graveside service for Father Murray. Father Isaac performed the eulogy. He called Father Murray a mentor, though Jacob knew for a fact the two were not close. Father Murray was to be his mentor, but that hadn't developed. Mostly, in Jacob's opinion, because of Father Isaac's reluctance to truly become a member of the community. Father Murray told him it was essential for the job. Father Isaac just ignored him, and treated it like just that, a job.

Edward gave a moving eulogy filled with stories and humor. Deep down, Jacob felt Father Murray would have appreciated it. It was how he had heard him speak of others that were friends that had passed on. When it was done, most didn't disperse or head back to some reception with the family. That was how funerals went in normal times, but these were not normal times. There were three services planned for today, and most just moved from one to the next. Jacob needed to be there for the first. Father Murray meant the world to him. He wasn't sure who was the second and headed back to the car and try to compose himself enough to make it through the third. More of those looks, and several whispers, greeted him as he passed people on his way back to the car. The looks bothered him enough, but what he heard ate at his core.

"He won't help," seemed to be the chorus that was repeated as people passed and looked at him as a complete deadbeat. By the time Jacob reached the car, he understood. These were the same people who looked at him as a savior before. Now they were in trouble, and where was he? He was the one not willing to even try. Jacob pounded the steering wheel in frustration. These people didn't understand, and they never would. His family had lost so much being what they wanted them to be, but it was all a big lie. Where the belief around town was the Meyers knew how to fix everything, the truth was they didn't. As more time had passed, Jacob believed more they were lucky when something worked and didn't make things worse, like what happened with Father Murray and Jacob's own grandparents.

Jacob also sat and played the events of two days ago in his head. In this instance, no one from their family had triggered or caused this, they just weren't able to stop it. Not that they had really tried yet. He wasn't sure what even caused it. Elmer Daughtry was there when he arrived, and there was no telling what he was doing before Jacob arrived. If he were to help, he would need to know that. Maybe one of his crew would know. Maybe Elmer had a go to activity. Jacob shook the thoughts from his head. He was not helping here. No more.

He took several deep breaths and attempted to settle his nerves before exiting the car again and making his way to the third and final service of the day. This one would be the hardest, and there was no way he could hide off in the trees for this one. He had to be front and center, in front of all the stares and whispers, but that wasn't the worst of it. His emotions shattered as soon as the two caskets, one shorter than the other, came into view.

Jacob froze, and his knees threatened to give way. As much as he tried to settle his nerves before, nothing could have prepared him for this. Tears were flowing before he even knew it, and the rest of the world melted away behind him. All he could see were the two oak boxes that held his family. The boxes that held everything that mattered to him. In their direction, he mouthed, "Sorry." Then he immediately hated himself for such a frivolous apology. He was sorry for what happened, sorry for not being able to stop it, sorry for not keeping them safe, but more than anything else, he was sorry for exposing them to this world. They were in those boxes because of so many of his decisions.

A hand gripped his, pulling him back to the present. He looked to his side and saw Alice. Her hand gripped his and then released and gripped it again. "You can do this," she whispered. It was the first kind whisper Jacob had heard all day. She led him up to the two caskets and to a row of empty seats which were at the front. He sat, and Alice sat next to him. Edward sat next to Alice. Father Isaac began, but Jacob didn't hear a word he said. There was no one else there with him, except those two boxes, and when Father Isaac was done, and the caskets lowered into the ground, Jacob was alone, and then it all crashed in on him. Off in the distance, the sky turned red, and the first creatures of the night appeared.

25

"Jacob."

"Father Isaac." Jacob greeted the young priest, but didn't invite him in. He stood in the barn's door, blocking it with his body.

"I want you to know, if you ever need anything, you can come talk to me. You have been through an enormous loss. It is natural to be upset, to feel anger, and to question your faith."

"Well, I thank you for stopping by Father. If I need anything, I will let you know." Jacob had one hand on the door ready to close it, but Father Isaac stood there like a man with more to say.

"Jacob, there is one other reason for my visit." He glanced back over his shoulder at the red sky behind him. Father Isaac's visit at this time of night surprised Jacob. His father would have braved what was going on, but not their young priest. He shied away from anything paranormal, and this was most certainly paranormal.

"I imagined there might be," Jacob said, almost taunting Father Isaac, who appeared to swallow hard before continuing.

"I know your father spoke to you. Jacob, we need your help."

Jacob held up a hand, which easily stopped the reluctant priest. "I thought I made myself clear yesterday, Father. This is not my fight, and even if it was. I don't have a clue how to stop this. Neither does my father."

Father Isaac flinched and looked up at Jacob, making eye contact for the first time since he arrived.

"That surprises you? Please tell me you haven't fallen for all the mysticism and pageantry. That book and cross are just symbols Father, that is all they are. Father Lucient himself told me that. What happens comes from the person, through the objects, and I got news for you. Those using them don't know anything. Trust me, I know. I was the only one here that was formally trained." Jacob leaned forward and winked at the man. He was pale. Jacob knew it had been a rough couple of days for him, and his age and inexperience didn't have anything to do with it. Even the most seasoned priest would be drained after two days straight of multiple funerals, with many more ahead of them. But there was something about how he stumbled backward when he heard what Jacob said that made it appear as though he had the wind punched out of him. He appeared so stunned that Jacob even asked, "Father, are you all right?"

There was a second hard swallow, and his voice had lost its previous strength. "Jacob, you and your father are men of incredible faith. Your faith in God, and your faith in each other. We have a lot of faith in you. That is the community and the church. I spoke with my superiors at the Vatican, and they have faith in you both."

Jacob let the door close behind him and leaned against the door to listen to what he felt was obviously a prepared and rehearsed speech.

"Your faith gives you strength, and I know you, and only you, are the one who can help us. I have called for help, and it is on the way, but they believe you are the best option. You mentioned Father Lucient. They say you were his best student."

"Good speech Father, but I am afraid they are just blowing smoke... in your face." Jacob may not have liked what Father Isaac said, but that didn't mean he was going to forget who he was, and adjusted the old saying, "... and you haven't really listened to anything I've said. Do you know our family's history and what all we have lost and how?"

He nodded.

"History repeats itself every generation, and I can't let that happen anymore. It ends here." The double meaning of his statement caused Jacob's lip to quiver for a moment before he pulled himself together. "I'm sorry if that disappoints you and my father, but that is what it is. Your help will arrive from the Vatican. We can only pray they have been holding out on us and truly know what they are doing. I know one thing for sure, I don't."'

Father Isaac turned and walked away, looking back over his shoulder at Jacob several times before he made it to his Prius. Jacob just stood there and watched, waiting for him to come back with a rebuttal. Hoping the priest had finally become one with this community and had developed a love for it and its people. At least enough of one to come and confront Jacob again face to face. That would show him it meant something, but there was nothing. Just the soft closing of a car door and the silence of a hybrid pulling off.

Jacob stood and watched it disappear into the darkness of the woods that surrounded his family's farm. Above that line of darkness hung a red sky with what Jacob called the devil's vultures flying around. There was no doubt they were terrorizing people, but what could he do about it? This was a momentary feeling of guilt for turning everyone who asked for help down. This was his feeling of helplessness talking. He truly didn't know. Not even an idea, good or bad, of where to start. This was new and on a scale unlike he had seen before. Maybe he had been a little over dramatic when he talked to his father and told him this was the start of the end of the world. Maybe he wasn't. Perhaps this was it. This was every verse in the book of Revelations all rolled into one. All that was needed now was the blowing of some ancient trumpet.

Like the night before, Jacob flipped through the five channels he had on the old console television. Tonight, it was really just four. The first station, an independent from nearby Falls River, was mostly static. Probably interference caused by something to do with the weather, or he hoped that was all it was. When he found something that was less annoying than the others, he laid back on his makeshift bed and tried to make the day go away, but every time he closed his eyes, he saw the same image. One that had been burned into his soul, and he was sure it would never leave. Two oak boxes with everything that mattered to him in them, slowly being lowered into the ground, while Father Isaac prayed. Friends and family wept all around, but Jacob didn't. There was nothing left, and crying wasn't an emotional response for where Jacob was. The only appropriate response for where he found himself was sitting there, feeling broken and considering if he could jump in the hole with them. Alice eventually helped him up. He remembered that much. He also remembered her saying bye to him at the car, but how he got home, he didn't remember.

After everyone left, and their whispers died down, he sat there frozen with a blank stare. He couldn't leave that place. Everything he cared about was there, and since the day he and Sylvia married, they had never spent a night apart.

The first night after her death, he stayed with her, against Todd Summer's better judgment, but his wife Mary brought Jacob a blanket and seemed to smooth things out. Jacob never slept. He just sat there in the chair that night until the sun came up before he headed back to the farm. He had every intention of taking care of the morning chores, but he only made it as far as feeding his dairy cows and then crashed in the barn.

Last night, he didn't push things with Todd and Mary. The night was torture. His mind roamed back to their bedroom, and he could have sworn she was right there next to him, but every time he leaned up to look or reached over for her, she wasn't there, sending him further down the hole.

Tonight, there were no delusions of her being there by his side. He knew where she and his son were, and it was both devastating and final. He would never see them again. He would never see their caskets again. He would never see anything of them again. Any pictures he had of them were nothing but ash. All he had were memories, but the only ones that played were the moment he found them lifeless on the ground, and the moment they lowered them into the ground.

Jacob spent hours trying to keep his eyes open, afraid of what his mind would show him when they closed. He eventually lost the battle. Just as he expected, it was nightmare after nightmare. Each startling him awake, screaming. Sometimes it was her name, sometimes it was in pain. Each time he tried to wage war on his eyelids again, but lost, and the images returned. Around four in the morning, Jacob wondered if death hurt, or if it hurt as bad as he was hurting now. His mind played with the various ways he could end it all right here in the barn, and there were many. His own exhaustion appeared to be all that was stopping him. That exhaustion finally took him, and no matter how horrible the nightmares that arrived were, or how empty he felt each time Sylvia slipped from his grasp, he didn't wake until someone kicked his bed.

"Jacob Meyer!" screamed the voice before there was another kick to the side of his bed. Jacob opened his eyes, and then shut them again, feeling this was another nightmare. That caused another kick to rattle the crates he called a bed. He opened his eyes again and rubbed the blurriness from his vision. Now he was wondering if he had died. Leaning over him was a rather religious and ominous scene. A nun flanked by two others. Behind them, a priest wearing the full black smock and red cape like he saw during his training at the Vatican. Jacob collapsed back onto his bed.

"Not now, sis."

26

"Yes now," she bellowed, and plopped down on the bed next to him, and held her bother. He hadn't felt a hug from her since his last visit with her before he returned home to Miller's Crossing. Since then, she had been through a lot. Losing Father Lucient, which affected them all, and her own trials. Jacob hugged her back. She buried her face against his neck.

"I am so sorry, Jacob. I am so sorry for Sylvia and Edwin. I wish I could have been here."

Jacob felt her tears running down her cheek against his neck.

Sarah kept mumbling, "I'm so sorry."

Jacob didn't want to let go. This had pulled him back from the edge of the abyss, slightly.

"Sis, what are you doing here?"

Sarah let go of her brother, but Jacob held on, and she quickly embraced him again before pushing away. Jacob propped himself up on his elbows, and looked at his sister, puzzled, then he looked at the others that were behind her.

"I would love to say I am here for you because of your loss, but in truth, I am here on official business."

"You're who Father Isaac called?" Jacob asked, surprised he even knew of Sarah. He seemed so disconnected from everything.

"Not exactly. He called his superiors, who talked with their superiors and so on and so on. They asked Father Rodrigo to come over and assist, and he brought me." She leaned forward. "I'm here to help you, little brother."

"We all are," said the priest. His accent was Italian, but not as thick as Father Lucient's.

Sarah sprung up off the bed and walked back to the priest. "This is Father Rodrigo. He took over for Father Lucient. Jacob, you really should get to know him. "

"Mr. Meyer, I'm at your service to assist and train." Father Rodrigo gave a little bow, and Jacob nodded in his direction, not sure what else to do.

"Sarah, have you talked to dad?" Jacob asked.

"Not yet, but we are planning to go there next."

"Oh," Jacob said. He got up out of bed, and then quickly grabbed the blanket of the bed to wrap around his waist. He had forgotten he slipped his pants off before getting into bed the night before and was only wearing his boxers. His sister snickered, but neither of the two nuns made any notice. Jacob needed to talk to his sister, but he needed to do so privately. She didn't know what had transpired between him and his father. "Sarah, can we talk? Privately?"

"Sure," she said.

Jacob motioned for the door, but no one took the hint. He did it again and wondered if head jerks were not an international understood. "Can you all step out and let me get dressed? Then we can take a walk around the farm."

"Of course." Sarah led the party out of the door.

Jacob quickly washed off using the workshop sink he had in the barn, and thew on some clean clothes his father had lent him. When he emerged, Sarah was walking around what remained of their old home while the others watched her. Jacob walked over and joined her.

"The bookcase would have been right there," Jacob said.

"I know," Sarah said. Her hands dug through the debris. "Remember that old family Bible? It should be in this area somewhere."

"Man, you sure are all in on this religious stuff," Jacob remarked. He glanced out of the corner of his eye to see if any of the others had heard him. It didn't seem they had.

"Yes, but that is not why I am looking for it. It has our family tree in it and shows the strength of our family. That makes it important to save if... we can." She threw two badly charred squares of something aside and then pulled out an enormous book. Even with the scorched cover, Jacob knew that was it. She laid it on top of the other debris and opened it. Other than some slight charring, the pages were undamaged. "See, our family is strong and can survive anything." She stood up and put it under her arm as she carried it out of the burned down home.

"Since when have you turned all philosophical?"

"Jacob, I've grown up and changed." She turned and looked at Jacob, who was still standing where the hallway that connected the kitchen and living room used to be. "Has it made me more philosophical, possibly? I have seen great suffering, but it is where great suffering exists that true strength is found."

Jacob saw the glint in his sister's eye and knew she was delivering a message directly to him. Now it was time for him to deliver a message to her. "Sarah, let's take a walk." Jacob walked out of the remains of the house and started out toward his fields. He glanced back at the priest and nuns that remained. "Don't they need to come with you?" He remembered the last time he saw her. Two nuns were always with her when she was awake, one always watching over her when she slept.

"Not so much anymore. They are more here for my comfort. We, it and I, have reached an agreement that has made life more pleasant."

Jacob froze and pondered what she said. Thoughts raced through his head, and he questioned if this was his sister speaking or it. She kept on walking and motioned for him to join her with her hand. When he did, she looped her arm around his.

"Relax, I have complete control, and just in case, they are not far. So, what is it you wanted to talk about? I have a feeling it isn't about what is going on here."

"Well, it is," he said sheepishly. "Sort of. See, dad's asked me to help him find the source of what is doing all this and help him stop it, but I said no."

Now it was Sarah who stopped. Her arm still looped around her brother's, and she yanked him to a stop. "Jacob Meyer! You have a responsibility here."

Jacob held up his hands. He wanted to stop her version of the same lecture he had heard now, twice. "I know. I know, but I can't. I know it might be hard to understand now that you are in the world you are in." His hand gestured up and down at the habit she wore. "But I can't. Sarah, this is all a farce. We don't know what we are doing, and mistakes after mistakes cost our family. Our grandparents died because of something our grandfather and Father Murray did wrong. Dad came back home and took up the cause, and..." Jacob hadn't had a problem citing this event to either his father or Father Isaac, but this time was different, and he struggled to find a more sensitive way to state it. "You know. Allowed the demon to find you." Sarah didn't even flinch. "And now this. This wouldn't have happened if they weren't part of my life."

Sarah reached over and grabbed her brother's chin. With force, she yanked it up of his chest so she could look right into the eyes of her brother, who was a few inches taller than her. "Jacob, knock off the self-pity crap. I'm not going to buy it."

"I..."

Jacob attempted to interrupt his sister, but she stopped that. "Nope. Nope. You had your chance to talk, now you need to hear me out. I remember Charlotte telling me all that nonsense about you not wanting to get involved with anyone because of what you might expose them to. Now you are letting those ghosts of those feelings blind you. Father Isaac told us twenty or more people have been lost since this started. Were you involved with all of them? Is there some connection between you and each of those that were lost? I'm going to answer for you. There isn't. The only connection is you all live in Miller's Crossing. And let me remind you, everyone here knows the dangers and risks. They can leave at any time, but they choose to accept them and help protect the secret." She let his chin go, but not without a quick rub of his cheek with her hand. "Jacob, you suffered a terrible loss. There is no denying that, and I can't imagine how you are feeling, but it's not your fault."

Jacob didn't agree, but he didn't argue the point with his sister.

"The emotions of loss are all of your emotions rolled into one. They just come at different times and intensities."

"Sarah, if you are going to quote the stages of grief to me, you can save it. Father Isaac has already given me that canned speech." Jacob resumed the walk.

Sarah joined him and again wrapped her arm around him. "All right, then why don't you show me your farm, and tell me what you know about what is happening?"

Jacob walked his sister through what were just empty fields the last time she was home. Now they were rolling fields of wheat, with a patch of tobacco. Something Lewis Tillingsly had talked him into. When he showed her his livestock, which was now up to thirty-nine head of grade-A dairy cows, he told her about Elmer Daughtry, the shed, and everything, which meant he needed to also back track several years to cover his last visit to the shed out in the Scar.

27

Jacob accompanied Sarah and her party to the church to meet with their father and Father Isaac. He offered to drive them in Father Murray's Cadillac, but Sarah took one look at that old thing and pointed at their nice new large rental sports utility vehicle they arrived in. Jacob couldn't decline, but did offer to drive as he knew the way.

They pulled into the gravel parking lot and found a space amongst the crowd of cars that were already parked there. Finding so many cars there on a Thursday morning both surprised and worried Jacob. Had something else happened? Jacob got out and started for the church. Hearing voices come from inside in a rather heated discussion hinted at what was going on. They often used the church for town meetings. This was probably one of those, and there was only one topic they were discussing, which also explained why he wasn't invited. He had been rather clear to his father, the sheriff, and Father Isaac he wanted nothing to do with it.

Jacob turned back to the vehicle. "Sarah, you guys wait here until I can figure out what is going on."

Stubborn as always, she said "Nonsense," and started for the church.

Jacob cut her off, grabbing her by both arms. "Sarah, you really need to wait. What happened back then, with you out at the Scar, is still an open wound for many in the community. I'm not sure how they would react."

"But Jacob, I can help."

Jacob shook his head. Hearing the raised voices inside the church, he knew she would walk into a powder keg, and she might just be what it took to ignite it. "Please," he begged his sister.

"Sister, maybe we should," suggested Father Rodrigo. He nodded at Jacob.

Sarah didn't say anything. She stood there with her hands folded together in front of her as Jacob headed to the church. At the top of the stairs, a thought hit Jacob like a cold slap. If word had gotten out about his reluctance to help, he might receive a similar welcome as Sarah. He braced himself and pulled open the door. The room went silent, and all eyes turned toward Jacob. He guessed the word had gotten around.

Without a word, he walked up the center aisle. His footsteps echoed in the silence. There were a few murmurs here and there, and he could hear most of what they said. It was sympathy, mostly from the more feminine voices. A few males greeted him with a "Jacob", or a nod. The rest watched as he passed.

Edward stood at the front with Father Isaac. Jacob wanted his father to meet him halfway, but he stayed put, forcing Jacob to walk the full length of the church. He stopped and bowed at the altar, a moment of respect that was more of a reflex than anything. He walked right up to his father and whispered, "Dad, I need to talk to you outside."

"Jacob, we are kind of in the middle of something," Edward said above a whisper.

"It's important."

A collective gasp ruptured the silence behind Jacob. The look on his father's face told him everything, and Jacob dipped his head. He had wanted to avoid this, but here it was. He turned around to see Sarah now standing in the doorway with two nuns busy in prayer on either side of her and Father Rodrigo behind them.

Edward hurried down the aisle and Sarah met him halfway. Jacob thought to himself, she is who he meets halfway. He threw his arms up and followed his father. The father and daughter embraced warmly in an ocean of fearful looks and pointing. Sarah had left a lasting impression on the community, and it wasn't a positive one. In a quick tally, Jacob noted five families present at this town hall that had lost a family member during her time out at the Scar.

Father Isaac rushed toward the father and daughter, looking concerned, almost fearful himself. Jacob had no doubt he had heard of Sarah. Most in their world had. "Perhaps we should take this to my office?" He all but pushed them toward the front and off to the side where his office was located. Jacob didn't see how this would work. He was in that office just two days ago and there was barely enough room for two, let alone seven. Father Isaac appeared to realize the miscalculation when he reached the door and froze.

"Perhaps your kitchen, Father?" suggested Edward.

There was a hesitation that his predecessor never showed. His kitchen, your kitchen, his front porch, your front porch, they were all his office. "All right." There was a reluctance in his voice and a slump in his shoulders as he led them to a place Sarah, Edward, and Jacob knew well.

Father Isaac had put his touch on it with several upgrades, which included replacing the old country chic table. Now there was something that appeared to have an endless amount of gloss coats applied on top of stained decorative panels. That didn't stop Sarah from taking her normal seat. Edward sat next to his daughter, still holding her hand. Her escorts positioned themselves behind them. There were two chairs left at the table, and Father Isaac promptly took one. Jacob offered the last remaining one to Father Rodrigo, who originally declined, but when Jacob offered again, he agreed, and Jacob took up a familiar position leaning against the country sink in front of the big window.

"Father Isaac called the Vatican, and they tapped Father Rodrigo to come and help. It was his idea to bring me along," Sarah explained to her father.

"Yes, your daughter is an expert in these situations."

"Expert," Jacob huffed under his breath. Everyone but his sister ignored him. She shot him an irritated look. Father Isaac hadn't taken his eyes off Sarah since he saw her.

Edward reached over and offered his hand to Father Rodrigo. "So, you replaced Father Lucient?"

"Replace? No," stated the priest rather matter-of-factly. He sat back in his chair and looked at the party around the table and then up at Jacob. "Father Lucient was a great man, a great priest, and a great Christian. I can only aspire to be like him, but I doubt I will ever achieve such a lofty goal. They have given me his charge, yes, but I have lots to learn, and your daughter here is a skilled teacher."

Sarah nodded and smiled proudly.

Father Isaac leaned across the table aggressively and asked, "Father, are you sure it was wise?" His finger pointed right at Sarah.

Without hesitation, Father Rodrigo answered. "I can understand you might have reservations, but I assure you, she is no more a danger to anyone than you or I. She has everything under control, and to be honest, we may all be safer with her here. She possesses a talent, that I am sure whatever is out there would not be fond of."

For the next twenty minutes, Father Rodrigo and Sarah recapped the events of the last several years of her life. Many of the details were ones she had held back, not wanting to worry her father and brother. With how Edward reacted, those omissions might have been wise. When Edward first heard, she let the Abaddon out in Lithuania; he sprung up out of his chair and leered across at Father Rodrigo. Father Rodrigo told him that had happened before he ever met Sarah. That was when Sarah told them all that it happened when Father Lucient died, and she possibly let emotions blind the logic in her decision-making process, but reminded everyone that it worked. Neither Jacob nor Edward shared her enthusiasm when she showed them the scar the cross caused when it hit her when she attempted to put him back in his place. Jacob saw where it was and realized what she was probably trying to do. His father didn't seem to make the connection, or at least didn't show it outwardly. He was too busy citing all the reasons it was dangerous for her to be here, and Father Isaac was quick to agree with every point.

She told of when she was put on trial, and the control Father Rodrigo taught her, but that didn't seem to sway their concern about her presence. When they ran out of arguments that amounted to adding her to the situation was like throwing fuel on a fire, Father Isaac went to how the community would feel and react. Jacob found it odd that the only time Father Isaac appeared passionate about what was best for the community was when it came to the presence of his own sister. This continued for several minutes, with Sarah deflecting or countering every point. She even slid over into the seat her father had sat in. This seemed to make Father Isaac uncomfortable, confirming Jacob's belief that he was afraid of her. It only ended when Father Rodrigo brought them all back to task.

"So, tell us about what is going on here."

"We don't know much more than what we told the Vatican over the phone," stated Father Isaac.

"Any idea on a source? Location?" asked Father Rodrigo.

"No. We have been looking, but so far nothing. What we are sure of, it's not in the Scar. I went out there yesterday to check. Nothing is out there, which is a problem in itself. The shed is gone. Its disappearance might have something to do with this, or not." Edward skewed his smile. "We haven't been out there since... in many years. So, we don't know when it disappeared. Maybe it's been gone for years. We just don't know."

Sarah looked right at her brother. Jacob knew what she was going to say before she said it. He felt the fear of the statement in his blood before the first word left her mouth, and he let his head dip.

"I believe Jacob knows."

All he could see was the floor, but he could feel everyone looking at him.

"Don't you?" she asked. It was a rhetorical question. Of course he did, and she knew it. Jacob had already told her everything. He did so in hopes she would understand why he doesn't want to be part of this anymore and hoped it would give her enough information to help.

"Jacob?" he heard his father ask.,

"I do," admitted Jacob. "The shed moved. It's in the woods off Willow Pine Road. That is where I found Elmer Daughtry three days ago."

"Three days ago," exclaimed Father Isaac.

Edward walked up to his son. "You found Elmer? Where is he now? Why didn't you say something?"

"One question at a time," responded Jacob, before walking toward the door that led to Father Isaac's dining room. "Yes, I found Elmer. I felt something and followed the feeling deep into the woods where I found the shed. Elmer was on the other side. As for where is he now? Well, he's dead. His body exploded on me when I tried to carry him out of there. It already had him. And before any of you ask me what it was, it's the same thing that was out there the last time I went out to the Scar. The thing I sat across the table with. Dad, you were right. You were completely right. I thought I ended things. I thought back then I was the big hero that saved the day, but you were right, as usual. That was just one battle in the eternal war. A blip in the sands of time, and so is this situation. Just another in a long line of events that have happened and will happen in the future."

"Jacob, why didn't you say something?"

"Dad, to save you," he said, exacerbated. "I was there when that thing exploded and shot those creatures into the sky. I saw what it could do. Sending you out there would be sending you to your death, and for what? For just another blimp in time, only for whatever this is to come back at some point in the future and have to be faced again. What's the point?"

"Jacob, the point is to protect and help! We have a duty to perform, and because you didn't say anything, people have died!" Edward's hands shook toward his son as he spoke. Jacob had never seen his father so upset, but that was not what had the most impact. His father had just spent the last two days telling Jacob Sylvia's and Edwin's deaths were not his fault. Now, he not only confirmed his belief, but also put the blood of everyone else who had died here firmly on his hands. Jacob felt it bubbling up again, but instead of letting it erupt out, he stormed out of the backdoor. His shoulder pushing his father aside as he exited.

28

Jacob exploded out into the area between Father Isaac's house and the church. He wasn't about to walk back inside where the town meeting was back in full swing. As he paced around, an attempt to walk off his anger and to outrun the guilt that was chasing him, he heard the new sheriff inside trying to keep control. Control of the people who were afraid. The people that looked to Jacob and his father to protect them. The people Jacob had let down and allowed their loved ones to die at the hands of those demonic creatures.

Every thought spiraled in the same direction, leading back to the same point, and while Jacob could accept it, he didn't feel he could live with it. Now he regretted not driving Father Murray's Cadillac here. If it were parked in the lot, he would have jumped right in it and taken off, driving as far as he could get on a tank of gas and never looking back.

"Master Meyer," a thick accented voice called.

Jacob stopped and let his hands drop. He gave them a few flexes to unclench the fists that were present at the end of them. The man behind him had not offended him, and even though he represented so much of what Jacob hated at this moment, he didn't want to disrespect him with any misguided hostility landing on him. "Father Rodrigo."

"Master Meyer, are you all right?"

"Yes, just drowning in guilt, I think."

"Heavy is the head that wears the crown," responded Father Rodrigo.

"I guess," Jacob said. Not exactly catching the reference. He recognized it as a song lyric, but something about Father Rodrigo didn't look like the traditional metal fan.

"It is a truth that cannot be avoided. Guilt is one of the many weights of responsibility, and in my opinion, it is the heaviest of all. It is the longest lasting too. Dread and fear pass quickly, but not guilt. It will weigh down every step you take, and every decision you make, and opens the door that its friends, doubt, second thoughts, and regret will come in."

"Okay, thanks," Jacob said, not exactly sure what Father Rodrigo was even talking about. It sounded rather prophetic, but Jacob didn't understand the point. He was reminding him of Father Isaac in that regard. He wondered if they taught a class at the Vatican on how to make something sound grandioso when it was really pointless.

"I'm sorry. I don't mean to overstep..."

"No," Jacob held up a hand to stop the priest. "It's fine. I'm fine." Jacob turned to walk back to the parking lot. He wanted to be alone.

"You're not fine," Father Rodrigo yelled after him. He was following Jacob, and that annoyed him. He was here to help the situation, not to be yet another person to tell him the obvious. "You're hurting deeply, and you feel lost, but mostly you feel betrayed."

Jacob turned and faced the priest, but kept walking backwards. "Betrayed? No disrespect, but you can save the theological based mumbo jumbo. I'm not interested in hearing how the lord works in mysteries ways. I've had enough." Jacob turned back around, hoping Father Rodrigo would take a hint. He had already resolved to just ignore him if he said anything more.

"You're correct. This is all just a bunch of what you call bullshit. All of it."

Jacob stopped and turned, but said nothing. His mouth hung open. He wasn't sure what surprised him more. The admission, or that a priest just said bullshit.

"Jacob, you are correct. None of us really knows what we are doing with all this. You, your father, me, or even Father Lucient, we all were just doing what we felt. Sometimes it worked, often it didn't, and we adjusted. What was important, though, was our faith–"

"You can stop there, Father. You almost had me. For just a moment, I thought you were making a real admission." Jacob turned and walked toward the parking lot. There wasn't a car there waiting for him, but it was the way out to the main road which Jacob intended to walk to and then walk all the way back to his farm.

"You misunderstand me, Master Meyer. Not your faith in God, but your faith in yourself. The faith in yourself to do the right thing. To want to help others. Your family was not just chosen because they could see ghosts. Many people can. What separated you and them was your willingness to use that ability for something great. Something greater than yourself." Father Rodrigo yelled after Jacob, which was music to his ears. That meant he wasn't following him anymore, which was just all right with him. "You don't believe you did the right thing, do you?"

"No, but I am now," Jacob yelled back with a wave of his hand.

"That is the grief talking Master Meyer. Don't dishonor their memory by not doing what they would have wanted you to do."

There were many things Father Rodrigo could have said that Jacob would have kept on walking in response to. This was not one of those. This was one that caused him to turn around and sprint back toward the priest. Father Rodrigo stood steady as Jacob stopped inches away from him with a finger extended. His nostrils flared, and every breath sounded like it came from some great beast.

"Don't... you... dare... talk... about.. them," Jacob huffed. He buried his finger further into Father Rodrigo's chest with every word.

"You didn't say I was wrong," Father Rodrigo responded calmly. "You feel guilty that you could not protect them. That magnifies your loss even more. And you find yourself angry at the world, especially the world you see as responsible for what happened."

Jacob backed away and gripped his head. His hands dug into his hair and then dragged down across his face, leaving red streaks behind. "If you are going to tell me about the phases of grief again, I am going to–"

"You are angry at the church, at your duty, but mostly you are angry at God."

Jacob stared right into Father Rodrigo's eyes and seethed, "Yes, I am angry at God. I am angry at everything."

"Good. That means you still care. Shall we have a seat?"

29

Father Rodrigo walked over to the trees that bordered the church property. Jacob stood and watched the man while he walked calmly, almost regally. He had seen that walk before. The quiet confidence. The peace in the face of hostility. Father Lucient walked like that, and if you took away the manicured dark hair on top of his head and replaced it with a mane of white, Jacob might forget who he was really watching.

There were no seats or benches in that direction, but at the base of a knobby old oak tree, he sat and leaned against the trunk in the shadows. A brisk breeze tousled the leaves above him. Jacob didn't know why, he could have continued walking out of the parking lot and start his way home, but he didn't, he felt compelled to follow the man, and join him, and that was what he did, picking the trunk of a neighboring tree to sit at and lean against.

Father Rodrigo did not address Jacob when he sat, and Jacob didn't either. There were no words. Just the sound of the world around them, peaceful. Something Jacob hadn't heard in the last few days. Since what happened, his world had been noisy, full of commotion, pain, and screams. All of it inside, none of it came from the outside after the first night. When Father Rodrigo finally spoke, it was just a simple question. "Feel better?"

The response was a simple nod.

"You are a lot like your sister. Stubborn, hotheaded, and passionate. You take a lot on yourself, and you don't give yourself any breaks. Things in your world are black and white. You succeed. You fail. It's never you did what you could. Jacob, living a life that way will only lead you to failure. You will always judge yourself by your biggest failure." Father Rodrigo looked over at Jacob. Before that, he was looking out in the field that separated them and the church. He appeared to wait for Jacob to say something, but Jacob had resigned himself to just listening. There was nothing more he could say. Satisfied there was no forthcoming response, Father Rodrigo continued. "It is true, all of this world you are part of is a guess. That is what life is. We make a guess, and we deal with the consequences. Do you go left or right on the road? Do you eat this or that for dinner? What profession do you choose? Do you stay close to home or leave? Do you stay close to friends? Life is all about choice, and those choices, as much as we try to convince ourselves otherwise, are just guesses. Some are more educated than others, but they are still guesses and those guesses come from the gut. We are creatures that are managed by feelings."

Father Rodrigo raised his right hand and then pounded the chest over his heart. "That in itself makes us both perfect and imperfect. We are imperfect because we rely on something so temperamental, something we can quantify, but at the same time it makes us perfect because our actions are because we are passionate and believe in something. That is also why we can't live in that black or white world of success or failure. Our failures are deeply personal because we failed in something we believed in. I love the church. I have dedicated my life to this, but I have failed. I have failed a great many times. Your sister tells me you are a farmer. I bet you have planted crops that have died, haven't you?"

Jacob shook his head. He hadn't. He had a few that went brown because of issues with his sprinkler system, but that was it. A quick fix had them back to health.

"No?"

Jacob shook his head again.

"Well, you will," said Father Rodrigo with a smile. "Nah, maybe you won't."

This brought a smirk to Jacob's face. The first in days.

"Jacob, this thing you and your family are part of is all a guess. You do what you believe will work. You trust the faith you have in yourself that it will, and that most of the time, makes it work. When it doesn't, you trust that same faith that you will find something that does. It's the same with your sister and all the Keepers. I wish it wasn't so. I wish it was more like hand-to-hand combat where we could train you, but even then, it's not a science. You still have to trust your training to deal with whatever your opponent throws at you. Sometimes you win, sometimes you lose, and it's easier to remember the losses more than the victories because of that weight. The weight of the guilt that hangs around your neck."

Jacob's hand reached up and rubbed his neck. Why, he didn't know. Maybe he was searching for the chain that weight hung from.

"Tell me about a time things went well?"

Jacob brushed it off with a hand wave and settled back against the tree. The silence he felt was heaven, and he wasn't all that interested in leaving it anytime soon. Though he doubted it would last long.

"Come on," urged Father Rodrigo. "I'm sure you have some stories."

Jacob thought for a minute. A few instances came to him, but none were story worthy. But the more he thought about them, they all were in their own right, so he picked one that caused a little wry smile to emerge. "There was this one time my father and I were called out to investigate a spirit that was roaming throughout a neighborhood behind the high school. We had to catch it first. It was fast, and not having to stay to dry ground, it didn't hesitate to lead us out through a boggy swamp. We were up to her knees in the muck, trying to keep up with it, but when it finally stopped, my father tended to it while I watched. Let's just say, whatever my father was saying wasn't music to its ears. That spirit flipped around on us so fast, we both fell back into the soup. He stood over us, glowing eyes, empty mouth, ear shattering screams, and all. I'm not going to try to make it sound like our lives were at risk. They may have been, I don't know, but I scrambled up to my feet and dad threw me the cross while everything that was alive in that swamp ran away around us. I went through the last rites prayer that was written in the family book. It was the only one I had used enough to have it memorized. He calmed down by the first line and was gone by the fourth. We came out of that thing covered in mud and decaying plants, and a stench that never came out of my clothes. I had to throw them away."

"So, it all worked out?"

"It did."

"But did you have any idea what you were doing?"

Without pause, Jacob shook his head and said, "Nah, not a clue." He hadn't realized it at the time, or maybe he had and didn't know enough to be concerned then. If they had known what they were doing, his father's attempt wouldn't have backfired.

"Then why did you do it? Why did you go out there in the first place?"

Jacob didn't have an answer to that question. Well, actually he did, and it was a simple one. They went out because someone called and needed their help, and it was their responsibility to help them. "Because someone asked."

"But wait, according to what you just told me, you didn't know what you were doing. Why would you rush out there to help? Or better yet, how did you know you could help?"

Jacob saw his point and didn't answer. He didn't need to. The answer was unspoken and floating in the breeze between them.

"You know I have counseled hundreds of individuals. Everything from people grieving a substantial loss and those with a personal loss of faith to the criminally insane that committed some of the most heinous crimes you can think of. Did I know exactly how to help each one of them before I met them? No, but I had faith I could help them. I knew I would do everything I could to help them. The same as you. We don't serve because we know how. We serve because we need to. It's who we are." Father Rodrigo stood up and left his tree to walk over to Jacob's. "I am not going to tell you I understand the pain and loss you feel. It is impossible for me to do so, that kind of pain is personal, but I can tell you I understand. I can understand what you feel on so many levels. Absolutely. One of those levels is that guilt of not stopping it and not only saving your wife and child, but everyone else too, and no matter how far you run from it, you will never escape that because it's who you are. You want to do everything you can to help others."

Father Rodrigo offered Jacob a hand, which he took and was helped up to his feet. His mind processing what he was just told, trying to deny that it was true, but he couldn't. It was all true.

"Master Meyer, with great power comes great responsibility."

"And our ability is that great power?" Jacob remembered Father Lucient saying something similar once.

"The ability that I believe you are referring to is a power, but not a great power. The desire to help is the greatest power you possess, and I'm afraid it's one that is rare in the world today. Everyone is focused on themselves. Very few consider the greater good. We need more like you. People need help today, and because you possess that desire, I'm afraid it falls to your responsibility, and you feel it."

"Did you just counsel me?" Jacob asked.

"In a manner of speaking, yes."

30

In the walk back to Father Isaac's home, Jacob had agreed to talk to the others about what he knew, but hadn't exactly come to terms enough to walk back out there and confront whatever this was. He understood completely what Father Rodrigo had said, and while he wouldn't really admit it to anyone, he agreed with it. He still had significant doubts regarding his future involvement in this side of the world. A point Jacob reminded his father of as they drove out to Willow Pine Road. Edward didn't attempt to argue. Instead, he quickly agreed and continued with more questions for Jacob about what they were about to walk into. Jacob told him everything he could and even added in information from the last time he was in that same shed, and sat across from It. To Jacob, this was a way to help, and as Father Rodrigo said, there was an abundance of people needing help, and not enough willing to help. Once this was all over, Jacob could find another way.

Both he and his father felt it as the procession of cars came closer to the spot Jacob had stopped at to make his way into the woods. When the vehicles stopped, Jacob hopped out and grabbed Sarah as she immediately headed for the woods.

"It's there. I feel it. We hear it." Her voice dripped with desire and that worried Jacob. He wasn't exactly sure who was talking at that moment.

"It is there," Edward stood, standing next to Jacob.

Father Rodrigo stepped forward and grabbed Sarah by the hands and led her back away from the side of the road. Both of her escorts gathered around her, kneeling and praying. Then he joined Edward and Jacob on the shoulder of the road. "I feel it too. There is a great evil out there."

"Now what?" asked Jacob. He looked at both men standing on either side of him. That was the question, and it was written all over both of their faces.

"We go in," responded Edward.

There was no question mark in his voice. No doubt in the answer. It was as sure and steady as if, well, if he truly knew what to do next, and that was when something Jacob's mother used to say came back to him. "Solve one problem, then solve the next." Of course, that advice was about his math problem, not trying to save the world. Going in was the first answer. What to do once they were there would be the second problem they would need to answer.

"Agreed, but give me a moment." Father Rodrigo walked back to their vehicle and opened the back and pulled out a black travel bag. He ripped the zipper open so harshly Jacob thought he heard the fabric rip. He reached in and pulled on what looked like two or three pairs of slacks, all black, that he placed on the ground next to him. Then his hand reached back inside and removed an object. One Jacob hadn't seen in a great number of years.

Father Isaac bowed his head as he saw the relic.

Sheriff Richards gasped.

Jacob could only stand and stare as he lifted the crown of thorns, Father Lucient's crown, and what he told them was Jesus's crown, up and placed upon his head. Jacob expected a loud thunderclap or something, but there wasn't. Just the silence of the world around them and, based on the position of the sun in the sky, they had about four more hours of that silence. Once the sun went down, this would be the epicenter of hell on earth. Jacob had already experienced it once, and he wasn't sure he wanted to be around for a second time.

"Let's go," Sarah said, and she marched toward the woods, but Father Rodrigo caught her by the arm.

"Sister, respectfully, why don't you wait here?"

She yanked her arm free from his grasp. "Not a chance. You need me in there." Her hand yanked toward the woods. "Remember Lithuania? Remember Turin? Remember Chile? You need us in there."

"Perhaps, but let me investigate first," insisted Father Rodrigo. "This place is connected to that beast inside you. The others weren't. It may not be safe."

"Father, you know I have control over it." Sarah appeared to leer at the priest, but when he held up his finger, she backed down quickly.

"Sister, I know you do, but again, remember, you are in my charge. This is my call. Let us investigate and if it is safe and we need you, I will send back for you." Father Rodrigo reached up and placed his hand on top of her head. "It will be fine." Jacob admired the quiet confidence the man exuded.

Sarah didn't flinch when Father Rodrigo removed his hand from the top of her head. She just stood there and watched as he walked to the edge of the road. Edward joined him, and then after a few reluctant glances around at the assembled group, Sheriff Richards and Father Isaac joined the two men.

Edward looked back at his son, and Jacob felt ashamed. He should be there with them, but he couldn't and even took a few steps backward and stood next to his sister. "You sure?" his father asked.

"Yes, I've seen it."

There wasn't another word between father and son. Edward turned around and the four men stepped off the road on to the ground. When Father Rodrigo's foot hit, the ground rumbled, and the trees rattled up high. Jacob took another step back. He had seen this show before.

"Dad, it's too dangerous," Jacob cried out.

Father Rodrigo and Sheriff Richards pushed through the underbrush. Before Edward stepped through, he turned and responded, "I have to. No one else will."

Jacob felt a sting and then despair when his father disappeared through.

31

Jacob stayed behind with his sister, and two nuns that kneeled beside her praying. His sister looked like the Sarah he knew, but she didn't act like the one he knew. She had changed. The old Sarah would have shoved Father Rodrigo to his ass and rushed right in. Now she stood there, hands folded in front of her, calm and stoic as she waited for word from the three men that left them a few minutes before.

He wished he could feel that calm, either on the inside or the outside, but that was an impossible ask. He paced around, making a few laps of the parked cars. Other times he walked right up to the edge of the road, never stepping off, and peered into the woods to see if he could see anything. Which he knew was a fruitless act. The shed was at least a thousand yards or more through some of the densest woods he had ever seen, and he could only see maybe twenty feet. He finally opened the door of the sheriff's cruiser and sat, with his leg propped up on the doorsill he sat and flipped on the radio, hoping maybe to hear some reports from him to the other deputies. The radio was quiet. Not that uncommon in Miller's Crossing. He flipped the laptop screen up on the cruiser's terminal, knowing he couldn't login. On the screen, the clock gave him the time. It had been exactly seventeen minutes since they entered. It felt like an hour. That prompted another quick check of the woods from the edge of the roadway, and just like the times before, Jacob couldn't see much.

After no updating, and seeing nothing but towering pine trees, Jacob turned around and headed back to the cruiser for another time and radio check when the world opened up behind him, throwing him to the ground in a flash of heat. Sarah bent into the wind and held firm, and her escorts stayed steady in their duty.

A quick push by his hands put Jacob back up to his feet and this time he headed to the woods, leaving the road. "Dad! Dad!" The answer was not his father. It was the moan and growl of a great beast deep in the woods. Deep in the direction of the shed, and Jacob had heard that sound before. He had sat across the table from it once before. He didn't think about it, his body just did as it reached in to pull the low brush out of his way so he could enter the woods.

"Jacob!" called Sarah.

He turned and saw her standing on the edge of the road. Both of her escorts were now sitting and silently watching her. "Stay there. I am going to go get them."

"Jacob," she called again.

"It will be fine," he said, and remembered all the times he told Sylvia that before he left out on some fool's errand with his father or Father Murray. It sounded even dumber now than it had before. Then there was an air of knowing what they were doing. It was false, but that was how people, Sylvia included, saw them. Jacob knew the truth and had talked openly about it. There was no secret to hide anymore.

He stepped in and started the journey to hell, but stopped after only a few steps. Figures were rushing toward him, and he couldn't quite make them out. His hand searched his pocket, but the object it desired wasn't there. He had turned it in to Father Isaac, who gave it to his father. With only a tree to hide behind, Jacob watched. The shape lumbered, falling from time to time. It didn't take long before the shape of three men, two men carrying another man, came in to view and he rushed to their aid. Father Rodrigo and Edward were carrying Sheriff Richards. All three men were battered and bloodied. Jacob attempted to check on his father, but Edward brushed him away. The three wanted out of the woods. Jacob pushed his father aside and took the weight of Sheriff Richards from both him and Father Rodrigo, and carried him the rest of the way out.

Sarah shrieked, "Dad!" upon seeing his shape when he stepped out and up to the road where he and Father Rodrigo collapsed. Now, in the sunlight, their injuries were worse than Jacob had initially seen. They were bruised and bloody, but also burned. With scorch marks on their arms and face. Sheriff Richards had a long branch broken off in his shoulder and appeared to have a broken leg. Jacob sat him down gently, and Sarah came over to check on him. Her escorts now tended to Father Rodrigo and Edward.

Jacob scrambled to the cruiser and flipped on the radio. "Sharon, it's Jacob. Get Ernie and Doc Wilson out here to Willow Pine Road. Sheriff Richards is hurt badly, and we have two others with severe burns, and Father Isaac is missing."

"Copy that, Jacob," her voice said without a crack. "Getting them out that way now."

He stood up out of the cruiser and looked up. The sky was changing right before his eyes. It was happening a lot earlier today. All Jacob could figure was they stirred something up. The three men were strewn out all over the road, being tended too, and were in no shape to go back in and fight. Jacob didn't think they would survive the arrival of the beast that flocked the skies at night.

"Jacob, ready?"

Jacob turned back toward the woods. Sarah stood there on the edge of the road, in her habit and all. She stepped off the road surface and on to the grass covered shoulder. The world screamed, rattling the ground beneath Jacob's feet. It was a painful scream, and his sister smiled before continuing forward to the woods. Jacob ran to his father, and pulled the wooden crucifix from his hand, and then followed his sister into the woods. He didn't know how this was going to go and he didn't know what he was going to do, but he wasn't going to give up without a fight, and at that moment Jacob finally understood all he needed to.

When they reached the clearing, Sarah stopped and stared at the shed. "I haven't seen that in years," she whispered.

"Are you okay?" Jacob asked. The crucifix in his hand was halfway up and ready to be pressed into her if needed. "If not, go back now."

Sarah punched Jacob in the arm. "I'm fine, but if your arm hurts, you can go back."

Jacob shook off the frog she gave him. "I want to check something." He motioned to go around the shed from behind. It was still burning under devious red flames that towered high into the sky, but there were no signs of the creatures. When they reached the other side, Jacob was quick to look around for anyone, or thing, that might be out there with them. He hadn't ventured this side or this far the last time. It didn't take long for him to find what he came around this side for. There, amongst the high grass and weeds, were a portable video camera on a tripod, a black bag, a ghost box, several electromagnetic force meters, and a Ouija board.

Sarah huffed and threw her hands up in the air when she saw the board.

"Bad memories?" remarked Jacob as he gathered the items into the black bag. Sarah just nudged her brother harshly in the side. "If we survive, maybe we can find out what happened here." He threw the bag over his shoulder and then solved the next problem. What next?

Next was finding out what was out there, and he led Sarah around to the front where he felt it would be best to do that. There were bits of Elmer Daughtry still over the ground. The door of the shed was open and while the outside was a burning inferno, the inside appeared calm and almost serene, with a single candle burning on the table. Ahead of them laid the decapitated body of Father Isaac. His own crucifix pinned his head to a nearby tree.

"We have to go inside," Jacob said.

"Inside? Are you sure?"

"Absolutely. I've done this before." Jacob walked up the dirt path to the porch. Sarah followed. Jacob stood up and waited for his sister before he moved toward the door. It was a good thing too. The door slammed shut as soon as Sarah stepped on the porch, and inside there was a roar that to Jacob almost sounded like the word, "No."

An invisible force sent Sarah rolling off the porch, but as soon as she stopped, she gathered herself and was back on her feet, marching toward the door. She countered the roar with a guttural, "Yes!" The door flew off its hinges and over Jacob's head, landing in a heap of splintered wood. She walked right past Jacob and threw the door.

Inside, Jacob found an eerily familiar scene. The table with two chairs on either side of each other, and a candle in the middle. This time, Jacob didn't sit, and when he felt a force pulling him toward the chair, he gripped the crucifix tighter.

"Show yourself," demanded Sarah.

"Now you don't want me to do that, do you?" responded a voice that still curdled Jacob's blood. The candle dimmed to just a tiny glow covering the table. Darkness cloaked the rest of the shed, and a layer of acidic smoke moved in, and with it, the putrid smell of burning flesh. "Jacob, there are always two. Don't think by bringing her back here you have tilted the balance of power in some way. There are still two of you and two of us here."

"Show yourself." This time, it was Jacob who made the demand.

"Have a seat. Let me hear a few more of your prayers." The seat across the table from them slid out and creaked. Jacob saw the dark form appear like before. Flames danced in its eyes. "What shall it be this time, Jacob? Shall we have another theological debate? I so enjoyed that last time."

"This time you have to deal with me," exploded Sarah. Her hands landed on the table with a thunderous boom.

"Oh, this could be quite enjoyable. All right. What shall we discuss?"

"How about why you are doing this, brother?" Sarah pushed Jacob out of the way and took a seat at the table. Her hand gripped his and pulled him close. There was something in her hand, and she passed it to him and then pushed him back away from the table. "And I'm not talking to Jacob. What is your point this time, brother?"

There was silence from the other side of the table, and Jacob looked down at his hand. Sarah had placed a closed vial in his hand. Holy water, if he had to guess. Her hand flashed around behind the chair and made a circle while pointing to the floor.

"Jacob, do you know why there are seven places around the world where the world of the dead cross with the world of the living? And here is a hint, it has nothing to do with seven continents."

"No, I don't," answered Jacob.

"What about you, brother? Do you want to tell him?"

"What is the point of all this? Sister Sarah Meyer," the voice said, carrying the smell of decayed flesh across the table.

"See, the number seven is very important in His world. Seven days, the seven statements that created the crucifix, the seven petitions of perfection, the seventy times seven is how many times Jesus said we are forgiven, but most importantly the seven demonic brothers. Each has their own place that they attempt to rule as part of the seven old kingdoms of the world. Isn't that right, Mammon?"

A deep groan echoed from across the table, and the chair creaked under the movement of a great weight.

"Relax brother, it's a stupid human belief that we can be dismissed by just knowing our name, but knowing it does make it easier to attack. What is it they say? Know thy enemy?" Sarah said. She turned in her chair and looked back at Jacob. "Did you study your demonology with Father Lucient?"

Jacob looked at his sister, who smiled widely back and then mouthed, "Circle all of us with that." The look on her face turned, and she sternly asked, "Well, did you?"

"Yes. Yes, I did. Mammon, the demon of greed, if I remember correctly."

"Very good," she said, and turned back around to face their host across the table. "Does knowing that tell you how you get rid of him?"

"Not exactly," responded Jacob, and he wasn't lying. He now knew what he was dealing with, but that didn't unlock any secrets for him. If anything, it might hint at the motivation, and Jacob could use that to figure out how, but there was no sheet that said when it is demon y, do x. Life would be a lot easier if it were, but the contrary was a well-established fact.

"See brother, you have nothing to worry about. So, what is the point of all this? This is your place. What more do you have to gain?"

"Existence only is unsatisfying," bellowed the beast.

"I can understand that."

Jacob was astonished by the seemingly casual conversation between two demons that was occurring right in front of him. Yes, one of them looked like his sister, but at the moment, he had no doubt that Abaddon was speaking at least part of the time. Jacob searched his sensations and still only felt one presence. Could Sarah's symbiotic state hide it from him? A question or research topic for later. He needed to get started on what his sister, or Abaddon, had instructed him to do. He popped the top off the vial and held it in his hand down by his side. Slowly, drop by drop, he let it fall to the floor, creating a complete arc with no gaps. Gaps would break the seal.

"Do you?" asked the beast. "You got what you wanted and now you are free to roam this world."

"I wouldn't call this freedom. We are all prisoners of some type. Me, in this form, controlled by this girl. You held to this place in a constant battle against those meant to oppress you. Even young Jacob back there, he is held prisoner by his sense of duty and his religious beliefs."

"Don't think I don't know what you are doing. Once the water dries, it will no longer restrain me."

Jacob was now behind the beast, suffocating in the stinging stench. He didn't stop, and the beast he now knew was Mammon didn't make any attempt to stop him.

"So, what would you do if you gained your freedom?" Sarah leaned across the table, interested in the answer, but her eyes followed Jacob as he rounded the table, almost done with the circle.

The question prompted a chuckle from Mammon. "Why, I would deliver freedom. Free humanity from the bounds of its stupid rules and laws. It would be a wonderful place."

Jacob finished the circle right behind his sister, and she twisted in her chair, turning it sideways to the table. It allowed her to lean even further across the table, but it also allowed her to reach back with one leg and use her foot to smudge out the circle. The leather on her shoe sizzled and small wafts of smoke rose up. She showed no signs of feeling pain or discomfort. Jacob was careful to put the top back on it when he put the vial back in her outstretched hand.

"It sounds it," Sarah stood up, and stepped back through the gap. "It sounds just like hell on earth!" With that, she held out her hand, and turned it, allowing a flow of holy water to fall to the ground, completing the circle.

The beast laughed until she splashed what she had left in its dark face. Flames appeared where it hit, and more putrid smoke filled the room.

"Move!" Sarah shoved her brother back through the open door. "He's right. As soon as it dries, he won't be restrained."

"Then why did we..." Jacob asked while he picked himself up off the ground outside the shed.

"To restrain him. To buy us some time. I learned something that will help." She pushed her brother back again.

"Stop it!"

"Sorry, I need some room."

"For what?"

Jacob found his answer, as the ground shook, a large tree fell on the shed. Then a second fell across it, forming, well... a cross. A third fell on another part of the shed, with a fourth falling across that one to create another cross.

"Duck!" screamed Sarah, and Jacob fell to the ground just in time as the tree behind him pulled free from the ground and floated over to the shed, where it became the stem for a third cross. Under it, the flaming shed was now just rubble, and most of the flames were snuffed out. A few wafts of smoke continued up, and Jacob saw two of the demonic flock attempting to form. Jacob stepped forward and held out the cross, hoping his sister wouldn't land a tree on him.

"Creatures I do not permit you in this world. You will leave in God's name." Both evaporated easily, and Jacob had wished it all had been that easy.

The remains of the shed rumbled under the layer of crosses.

"Jacob, I need you to focus everything you have on that. We are going to do what is called a seal. Something I saw in Lithuania."

"What do I do?" asked Jacob.

"Use your best protection stuff, and bless each of those crosses," responded Sarah.

Jacob's eyes looked up high in the trees where each of the trees that surrounded the clearing were being added to. Trees from the next rows were being sacrificed and slammed across them, joined to create crosses.

"Jacob, you need to get started now!"

He approached the closest cross lying across the shed and pressed his family's crucifix against it. "Heavenly Father, allow your light to flow through this object as a symbol of your greatness in both this world and in heaven. Use it to protect us, your faithful servants, allowing us to live free from temptation of sin while delivering your good word. Amen." Before Jacob finished, his cross glowed, and that glow propagated up along the cross he had pressed it against. Before his eyes, the bark covered cross turned gold. He expected it to dissipate and once again become a bark covered tree, but it didn't. It stayed golden. As did the next four that lay across the shed's rubble. When he was done with those, Sarah directed him to start on one side of the clearing, repeating it for every cross.

EPILOGUE

Wounds, both physical and emotionally healed. Even some wounds from the past were made less painful when word got out about who helped bring this latest event to an end. Sarah was sure to give all the credit to her brother, humble to the end. Jacob tried to set the record straight, but Sarah pulled him aside and told him the town needed to believe in him, not her. He understood what she meant, but he didn't like it. That was the first of many things that occurred over the next several months that Jacob found he wouldn't like, but would have to accept.

The burns suffered by his father were severe and limited his involvement in any future "family" responsibilities. Jacob completed the map, by himself, but made sure to review the final product with his father to cross reference with his notes and knowledge. The new location of the shed was marked with a big red 'X' and had become the second forbidden area in Miller's Crossing. Jacob visited both locations weekly to check their current status, to see if the shed ever moved back, or disappeared. He would do so for the rest of his life.

Sarah left six weeks after the seal was placed. That was when Father Rodrigo was able to travel. She never went with Jacob out to either place. Jacob felt it was too risky, and Sarah didn't protest too hard. She stayed in Father Isaac's place, a suggestion from the Vatican. The ground was holy and would serve as added protection. Father Rodrigo told them such precautions weren't needed, but they insisted citing his current condition as a concern. It was roomier and had better creature comforts than anything Jacob could have offered her. He only had a barn.

After a few days, Alice convinced Jacob to leave his rather rustic habitat, and move in with her and Edward until the farmhouse could be rebuilt. Jacob wasn't sure if it ever would. It needed to be, but there were memories, and doing anything to the remains of the original home threatened to destroy them.

The first Sunday since the peace was restored arrived, and people gathered at the church as usual. Father Rodrigo attempted to conduct a service, but pain caused him to sit often, and take breaks. Sarah stepped in to help. Some were accepting of this, while others stood up and walked out with a few grumbles.

By the second Sunday, a replacement priest arrived, but by that Sunday afternoon he had packed his bags and left. His first sighting of an actual spirit seemed to force the holy spirit from him, and he took off running. It was only a few days later the next one arrived. If Father Isaac was clinical in his approach to the community, this one was sterile. Father Robert Tyson, a man of almost forty, with several lengthy assignments under his belt. Jacob arranged a greeting for him with several of the town elders. They all showed, except Father Tyson. Jacob went out in search of the Father and found him in his office, working on the sermon for Sunday. When Jacob told him of the meeting, and asked him if he forgot, he said the meeting wasn't important and immediately went back to what he called, "God's Word."

The sermon was a world is ending, fire and brimstone, fear packed, ideological monologue. Jacob sat there listening for a theme. Halfway through it he leaned to Father Rodrigo and asked if he knew where this was going. He didn't have a clue. After the service was over, he led the procession out of the church and disappeared. There was no one there to greet and speak with the parishioners as they exited.

The Vatican agreed to replace this one at Father Rodrigo's request, but they couldn't provide a timeline for when that would happen. When the next Sunday arrived, the seat was still vacant, and Father Rodrigo attempted to fill in again, but his condition was still an impediment. Sarah attempted to help, but when the grumbles started again Jacob intervened. A few were walking out, when Jacob asked for them to wait. He then walked up to the same pulpit that Father Murray had occupied for over fifty years. He reached for his sister's hand and led her down to the pews in the front where she sat with her escorts. From there he finished the reading, which led to today's sermon, and all eyes were on him.

Jacob stood there for a second, the focus of dozens of eyes, but he didn't feel uncomfortable. Why would he? These were his people. The people of his town. The people he had grown up around since a very young age, and the people he felt driven to help however he could. "Today, let's talk about something we all know a lot about, whether we want to know about it or not, healing..."

No further replacements were sent by the Vatican.

Ready for what is next for the Meyer's Family?

Dear Reader,

Thank you for taking a chance on this book. I hope you enjoyed it. If you did, I'd be more than grateful if you could leave a review on Amazon (even if it is just a rating and a sentence or two). Every review makes a difference to an author and helps other readers discover the book.

While this is the end of Miller's Crossing, it isn't the end for the Miller's Family. There is a spinoff series following Sarah Miller and her adventures. I have included the first chapter of book one in that series below.

As always, thank you for reading,
David

P.S. Signup for my readers list and I'll send you my monthly list of free offerings from other authors and notifications of my new releases: www.authordavidclark.com. You will receive the Miller's Crossing prequel – The Origins of Miller's Crossing – for free, just for joining.

DAVID CLARK

THE STORIES OF SISTER SARAH

1

"First, I want to thank you for agreeing to meet with us."

The old woman sat upright in a simple wooden chair with a pleasant look on her face. A man, only a few years younger than her, sat off to her left. He was apprehensive and sat on the edge of his chair as if he were ready to pounce on some great evil at any moment. Looking at the tone of his senior-citizen body, it was obvious he could still do that if needed. He had every appearance of someone who knew a life of manual labor. Maybe a craftsman or a farmer. On either side of the woman's chair, two nuns knelt and prayed silently.

"Oh, not at all. I am more than happy to talk about my life. You will have to excuse my brother, he is a bit protective of me."

"Well, I hope to put him at ease. We are here with all due respect, and hope to conduct this interview as such. Your Mother Superior gave us an hour, shall we begin?"

The young man who had been speaking leaned forward just a bit further and placed a microphone on the floor in front of the elder nun. His black-rimmed glasses almost slipped off his nose when he bent over, prompting a quick push back into place with his forefinger. The hand continued to brush a mop of straggly-length dark hair out of his face.

"Any background?", he asked the blonde twenty-something to his side. The man gave him a thumbs up.

"First, can you introduce yourself and tell us who you are?"

"Sure, I am Sarah Meyer. Daughter of Edward Meyer."

"And, you are a nun here at San Francesco?"

"In a way of speaking. They take care of us, and I follow their beliefs and life. I must admit, I found the life very pleasing and finally took the oath when I was thirty-three."

"And how old are you? If you don't mind me asking?"

There was a great pause between the six people in the room, only the two nuns continued. Their prayers nothing more than a whisper.

"Not at all, I am 85 years old, and IT is 3184 years old."

One of the two nuns gasped out loud and paused her prayer for only the briefest of moments. Sarah looked in her direction and said with a calm voice,

"Please don't stop child. I don't want it to make a mess of these nice men. I have a story to tell."

There were two audible gulps in the room, and Jacob leaned forward further in his chair. Sarah extended her hand out toward her brother and placed it on his knee. She smiled rather mischievously. Not like someone who was evil, but more like someone who was having a little fun. Which was the case. At this moment, she felt in complete control of herself. The two younger nuns, both relatively new when compared to her length of stay, were doing a fine job of keeping Abaddon hidden, as did all the sisters that had served at Sarah's side. There were only brief moments where she lost control. All brought back under control without any world-ending catastrophes. A welcome improvement over the first time he took control of Sarah.

"You gentlemen can relax. We are perfectly fine at this moment, but let's not waste time."

"Yes ma'am. We don't want to cover what happened before you arrived here. We have already spoken to your brother about that, and that has been well documented many times over once the story came out."

Sarah chuckled, almost a grandmotherly laugh as if a grandchild amused her, but it came across as disturbing and, once again, set the tense room on edge. "Oh, I am sorry," she apologized. "I don't know why, can't really explain it, but thinking about how our secret was let out still amuses me. Maybe it was how hard everyone worked to keep it a secret, but in the end the Vatican published a book on us all. No investigative exposé or anything, just a book all on our own."

"Yes," he stumbled. "It is a wonderful book. I have read it many times. The section on you and your family is fascinating."

"I have read it too. The missed quite a bit, but that is expected. Please continue."

"What we are most interested in are the stories once you arrived here. The, I guess, cases you helped Father Lucian and the other keepers with through the years, using.. ITs power."

"I imagined that was what you would want to hear. I helped him with a great many, up until his passing, and then Father Domingo took his place and we continued our work. Is there a particular one you want to hear about first?"

He consulted his notebook, flipping through several pages of scribbled items. Sarah thought, *how old school of him, he still writes notes.* Most of those that have come and talked to her walked in with a digital notebook or robotic camera. Not these two. The main interviewer, a man in his mid-thirties she would guess, in a brown sweater almost has that documentary film student look, with his pad full of notes. She bet, and before she finished the thought, her eyes found the pencil stuck behind his ear. During the vetting process, something Jacob always did, he verified these two were not just students, or anyone that might be there to exploit her. They were professionals, two of the best. Ralph Fredricks, and two-time Golden Globe winner, and his cameraman Kenneth Lloyd. Sarah hadn't had a chance to watch any of the films they produced, but she trusted her brother. She was aware of the sheer number that he had turned down since the book came out fifteen years ago.

The book, something no one warned anyone about, was aimed at trying to return the world's faith in the spiritual. Pope Mark, a priest from Columbia, said he felt like he was watching the world walk away from God and toward the digital spark of technology, forgetting who they really were and where they came from. It was a theme in every sermon he gave. It was also dead center of his policies and directions from the Papal office. A media campaign, unlike any the church had undertaken, began to show the world the spiritual side they had forgotten. Movies and shows about religious sites and figures. The reception was lukewarm. His critics within the church said the stories were old and worn. Everyone knew the figures. Everyone knew the sites. None of them had any appeal.

Then, through several edicts and Papal papers, he began to acknowledge the church's belief in the paranormal, and the truth about its support in the practice of exorcisms. Both were expected to make a splash, but they didn't do much more than create a ripple. Popular culture movies and themes had desensitized the entire world to those topics. In what some called an act of desperation, he outed the Sites, the Keepers, and all their stories. To Sarah's horror, there was no warning when it was released. Mother Francine woke her early one morning and told her as soon as she had heard herself. That was the first. She lived in fear for a while, and stayed secluded in her room. Not even taking the walks out among the trees in the courtyards to listen to the birds, an activity she had grown very fond of through the years. Sarah knew some details of her story were not as glorious as others, and might even make her the target for both those wanting to grab a piece of story, and those that would fear her and want to protect the world from her, but no one came. No one inquired. The public dismissed the stories as works of fiction. Then little by little, a few interviews with keepers here and a documentary there, credibility grew. That created a ground swell which turned into a tidal wave of requests. All of which the Abbey diverted to Jacob, who eagerly volunteered so they wouldn't be bothered. It was a burden he explained he needed to do after all they had done for his sister.

"Sister, how about the first time?" Ralph asked, after closing his notebook.

"How did I know you would ask about Poveglia?"

"It is called the most haunted place in the world, and it was your first time," he responded.

"Well, then. Let's get to it."

ALSO BY DAVID CLARK

doesn't stop them from turning to him when they come across something that the natural world can't explain, such as the mysterious death of a coed in Richmond Virginia. They sent Jordan up to just consult on her autopsy, but her spirit begs him to dig further. With Megan's help, they uncover a ring of evil that spreads up to the highest reaches of government, and cost several young women their lives to keep them silent. What is the old saying, dead men tell no tales? Well that is true, unless you have someone who can speak to the dead now isn't it? Together the hunt down those responsible and try to stay out of the way of their only true adversary, an entity who says he is the source of all Evil in the world.

The Dark Angel Mysteries

The Blood Dahlia (The Dark Angel Mysteries Book #1)

Meet Lynch, he is a private detective that is a bit of a jerk. Okay, let's face it he is a big jerk who is despised by most, feared by those who cross him, and barely tolerated by those who really know him. He smokes, drinks, cusses, and could care less what anyone else thinks about him, and that is exactly how the metropolis of New Metro needs him as their protector against the supernatural scum that lurk around in the shadows. He is "The Dark Angel."

The year is 2053, and the daughters of the town's well-to-do families are disappearing without a trace. No witnesses. No evidence. No ransom notes. No leads at all until they find a few, dead and drained of all their blood by an unknown, but seemingly unnatural assailant. The only person suited for this investigation is Lynch, a surly ex-cop turned private detective with an on-again-off-again 'its complicated' girlfriend, and a secret. He can't die, he can't feel pain, and he sees the world in a way no one ever should. He sees all that is there, both natural and supernatural. His exploits have earned him the name Dark Angel among those that have crossed him. His only problem, no one told him how to truly use this *ability*. Time is running out for missing girls, and Lynch is the only one who can find and save them. Will he figure out the mystery in time and will he know what to do when he finds them?

Ghost Storm – Available Now

There is nothing natural about this hurricane. An evil shaman unleashes a super-storm powered by an ancient Amazon spirit to enslave to humanity. Can one man realize what is important in time to protect his family from this danger?

Successful attorney Jim Preston hates living in his late father's shadow. Eager to leave his stress behind and validate his hard work, he takes his family on a lavish Florida vacation. But his plan turns to dust when a malicious shaman summons a hurricane of soul-stealing spirits.

Though his skeptical lawyer mind disbelieves at first, Jim can't ignore the warnings when the violent wraiths forge a path of destruction. But after numerous unsuccessful escape attempts, his only hope of protecting his wife and children is to confront an ancient demonic force head-on... or become its prisoner.

Can Jim prove he's worth more than a fancy house or car and stop a brutal spectral horde from killing everything he holds dear?

Game Master Series

Book One - Game Master – Game On

This fast-paced adrenaline filled series follows Robert Deluiz and his friends behind the veil of 1's and 0's and into the underbelly of the online universe where they are trapped as pawns in a sadistic game show for their very lives. Lose a challenge, and you die a horrible death to the cheers and profit of the viewers. Win them all, and you are changed forever.

Can Robert out play, outsmart, and outlast his friends to survive and be crowned Game Master?

Buy book one, Game Master: Game On and see if you have what it takes to be the Game Master.

Book Two - Game Master – Playing for Keeps

The fast-paced horror for Robert and his new wife, Amy, continue. They think they have the game mastered when new players enter with their own set of rules, and they have no intention of playing fair. Motivated by anger and money, the root of all evil, these individuals devise a plan a for the Robert and his friends to repay them. The price... is their lives.

Game Master Play On is a fast-paced sequel ripped from today's headlines. If you like thriller stories with a touch of realism and a stunning twist that goes back to the origins of the Game Master show itself, then you will love this entry in David Clark's dark web trilogy, Game Master.

Buy book two, Game Master: Playing for Keeps to find out if the SanSquad survives.

Book Three - Game Master – Reboot

With one of their own in danger, Robert and Doug reach out to a few of the games earliest players to mount a rescue. During their efforts, Robert finds himself immersed in a Cold War battle to save their friend. Their adversary... an ex-KGB super spy, now turned arms dealer, who is considered one of the most dangerous men walking the planet. Will the skills Robert has learned playing the game help him in this real world raid? There is no trick CGI or trap doors here, the threats are all real.

Buy book three, Game Master: Reboot to read the thrilling conclusion of the Game Master series.

Highway 666 Series

Book One – Highway 666

A collection of four tales straight from the depths of hell itself. These four tales will take you on a high-speed chase down Highway 666, rip your heart out, burn you in a hell, and then leave you feeling lonely and cold at the end.

Stories Include:

- Highway 666 - The fate of three teenagers hooked into a demonic ride-share.
- Till Death – A new spin on the wedding vows
- Demon Apocalypse - It is the end of days, but not how the Bible described it.
- Eternal Journey - A young girl is forever condemned to her last walk, her journey will never end

Book Two – The Splurge

A collection of short stories that follows one family through a dysfunctional Holiday Season that makes the Griswold's look like a Norman Rockwell painting.

Stories included:

- Trick or Treat – The annual neighborhood Halloween decorating contest is taken a bit too far and elicits some unwilling volunteers.

- Family Dinner – When your immediate family abandons you on Thanksgiving, what do you do? Well, you dig down deep on the family tree.
- The Splurge – This is a "Purge" parody focused around the First Black Friday Sale.
- Christmas Eve Nightmare – The family finds more than a Yule log in the fireplace on Christmas Eve

A big thank you to my beta reading team. Without all your feedback, books like this one would not be possible. Thank you for all your hard work.

ABOUT THE AUTHOR

David Clark is an american author who is both traditionally and independently published. His works span the horror, thriller, and science fiction genres and includes the international bestselling paranormal series "The Ghosts of Miller's Crossing".

You can follow him on social media.
Facebook – https://www.facebook.com/DavidClarkHorror
Website – https://www.authordavidclark.com
Twitter – @davidclark6208